Auden kissed back, eyes closed.

It was moments like this where he believed, almost believed, that this was more than just a fuck. He'd told himself enough times that he and Trayce were just friends, teammates, two guys who sometimes spent their evenings naked and sweaty together. Nothing more. And that had been fine, a few months ago, but a sense of normalcy was lacking in everything Auden did these days. Just once, he'd like to know what it felt like to be a normal twenty year old kid.

"My turn," Trayce murmured a moment later, stepping away from Auden and tugging him towards the bed by his shirt.

"I have to go," Auden said reluctantly, glancing at the alarm clock on Trayce's desk. A part of him didn't want to leave, not when there was the possibility of getting Trayce naked and on his back, vulnerable to him.

Trayce dropped his hand and shrugged. "If you have to. Or you could get over here and take your clothes off."

Auden couldn't suppress his smile as he shook his head. "Fuck you." He'd deal with Anya's annoyance at his lateness later. Right now, he had a smug Trayce to take care of. Stepping forward, he shoved Trayce's chest and Trayce fell backward onto the bed.

Also recommended...

You may also enjoy these other Forbidden Fiction works:

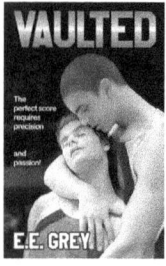

Vaulted by E. E. Grey
Dorian has been working his whole life to make the Olympic gymnastics team and win that elusive all-around gold medal. Just because he's the youngest, shortest and not the most socially savvy team member shouldn't warrant all the teasing — bullying, really — he has to endure, especially from Jules Gardner, the former Olympic bronze medalist and current teammate. He's had a crush on Jules for years, but Dorian isn't going to let Jules get in the way of his goals, no matter what.
http://forbiddenfiction.com/story/EEG-1.000138

Slow Surrender by Olivia Stone
Lucas Walker is a barista by day and a drag queen by night, working toward making a name for himself in Los Angeles. Everything seems to be falling into place, except in the romance department. The guys he's met so far don't seem to understand that just because Lucas does drag, that doesn't mean he's submissive. Lucas is looking for someone he can push and challenge, someone who truly wants to submit. When Connor walks into the drag bar one night, Lucas thinks he may have finally found what he's looking for.
http://forbiddenfiction.com/story/os2-1.000211

Tumbled

E. E. Grey

ForbiddenFiction
www.forbiddenfiction.com

an imprint of

Fantastic Fiction Publishing
www.fantasticfictionpublishing.com

TUMBLED
A Forbidden Fiction book

Fantastic Fiction Publishing
Hayward, California

© E. E. Grey, 2016

CREDITS
Editor: James L. Wolf, Lon Sarver
Cover Design: Siolnatine
Cover photo: Jeannie Bell
Production Editor: Erika L Firanc
Proofreading: JhP323 andKailin Morgan

SKU: EEG-000156-02 FFP
ISBN: 978-1-62234-283-9

Published in the United States of America

DISCLAIMER

This book is a work of fiction which contains explicit erotic content; it is intended for mature readers. Do not read this if it's not legal for you.

All the characters, locations and events herein are fictional. While elements of existing locations or historical characters or events may be used fictitiously, any resemblance to actual people, places or events is coincidental.

This story is not intended to be used as an instruction manual. It may contain descriptions of erotic acts that are immoral, illegal, or unsafe. Do not take the events in this story as proof of the plausibility or safety of any particular practice.

For Anne, who will never read this.

Contents

Chapter 1
Opening the Gateway

December 2023

World Gymnastics Championships
Antwerp, Belgium

Auden posed for yet another photograph, holding the gold medal slung around his neck. He wasn't sure it was ever going to end, but he grinned for the camera. Around him, other competitors milled under the banner of the annual World Championship 2023, showing off their medals and taking more pictures as well.

Searching the crowd, Auden looked for his coach, but he couldn't find Dorian amongst the mess of reporters and winners. It felt like the last couple of days had been a complete blur, from arriving in Antwerp for the competition to being named World Champion pommel horse. He almost felt as though he'd missed it all despite being in the middle of it.

He was caught off guard as Trayce bounced up to him and grabbed him into a crushing hug. He could feel every place their bodies touched, warm and solid pressed together. Trayce's dark brown hair tickled his neck and he hesitated to let go, but the hug didn't last long enough.

"Look at that!" Trayce grinned, stepping back. "We're medal twins." He dusted off the gold medal around his neck. "Dorian's probably already dreaming of Olympic trials in June. Imagine two Olympians from the same Center. I think he would die."

Auden smiled at Trayce, missing the warmth when Trayce

pulled away. "He's too young to have a heart attack."

Trayce bounced on the balls of his feet, looking too hyped to control himself. It was a change from his usual calm demeanor that Auden had grown used to in the past few years training together. He knew what caused it, though — it wasn't just being a world champion; it was what came after.

"We can only hope we both make it. Don't think this medal makes you any better competition, Auden. I plan on crushing you in trials." Trayce's grey eyes glittered mischievously as he laughed. As much as Trayce looked like every other gymnast in his physique — defined arm muscles and a six-pack — he had a thin face, a few freckles on his arms, and a nose that looked as though it had been broken a few too many times.

"We'll see about that."

Trayce stopped his bounce to meet Auden's eyes, lingering for a second, and the heavy thing in Auden's stomach fluttered nervously instead. Leaning forward, Trayce grabbed his shoulder for a fleeting moment, giving it a squeeze and lowering his voice.

"Come to my room later and we can celebrate our wins." He grinned slyly at Auden before releasing him and seeking out another teammate.

Letting out a breath, Auden didn't watch him go. There was no doubt what would happen in Trayce's room later, but he had to focus on the moment right now. He wanted to enjoy it. It wasn't every day that he won a gold medal. After so many years of work, it was finally paying off.

"Auden." Dorian appeared out of the crowd, looking ruffled, blond hair mussed as though he'd been running his hands through it out of frustration. He pulled Auden out of the way of the photographers with a scowl. Auden knew Dorian had never been a fan of the press. "Good job today. You should be proud."

Auden fingered the medal around his neck and nodded. "Thanks."

"And you know," Dorian went on, leading him out of the crowd. "That this is only the beginning. A medal at World's paves the way to the Olympics. Trials are in June which means we've only got six months to make you the best of the best. It's time to buckle down."

Auden laughed. "Like we haven't already."

Dorian didn't smile which made Auden's fade slightly. "The Olympics are serious competition. Everyone there is the best and you have to be better. This is what you've been working towards. Now is not the time to get cocky. As soon as we get back to Phoenix, we'll be working harder and longer on your routines. Are you ready to put in everything?"

It was a stupid question considering where he was. He'd just medaled at the world championships. Trials were right around the corner—he'd be an idiot to give up now.

He nodded finally, and Dorian clapped his shoulder.

"Good, 'cause I expect to see you on that team come July."

Auden sighed as Dorian left. His whole life would change in the next six months, and it started now.

April 2024

Elite Gymnastics Center
Phoenix, AZ
Two Months to Olympic Trials

The blood rushed to Auden's head as he held his handstand, counting to three before coming out of it and going into a double pike that sent him spinning off the mat, air rushing past him as his feet hit the ground and bounced back up again. Sweat beaded on his brow as he backed into the corner for the final jump.

Taking off, he took a skip before launching into the salto, soaring off the mat and landing with barely a bounce at the other end of the mat. He let out a breath as he trotted off the mat to grab his towel. Not bad. On the bench, Anya gave him the thumbs up from where she sat braiding her thick blond hair.

The gym rose high over his head, the ceiling hung with bright fluorescent lights that made it seem like high noon, no matter what the time of day. Most of the floor was covered in thick, blue mats, with thicker mats in varying colors piled against the walls for practicing new jumps. A pommel horse was set up in the far corner, next to the long runway to the vault. The girls' team was working on the bars and beam that day, on the other side of the gym.

"Auden, we need to talk."

There was no other sentence in the English language that could make Auden's stomach drop the way it did when Dorian pulled him off the mat. For a moment, he wracked his brain, trying to come up with his mistake—what had he done wrong in the routine? Stepped off the mat? Over-rotated? Didn't hold the handstand long enough?

Dorian tugged him to the side, nodding for Liam to start his routine next. One of the assistant coaches followed him to the mat, but Dorian turned to Auden.

Auden hadn't been training under Dorian for very long, barely three years, but he knew Dorian took everything seriously. If he'd done something wrong, he was about to hear about it. Dorian's expression was enough to make nerves swell in his chest. Talks like that were something Auden tried his best to avoid if at all possible.

"Yeah, Coach?" he asked instead, plucking at the hem of his tank, trying to appear unconcerned, but inside, his heart thudded loudly.

"I've been looking at your routine," Dorian said finally, arms crossed and lips pressed together. "A few of your routines, actually. I think they need some work. You're not pushing yourself hard enough." He shook his head at Auden. "Your routines are fine, but the difficulty levels just aren't there, especially for someone of your skill level. You just did two pikes in that routine, but a double-twist double-back would be a step up in difficulty which will give you a higher top score, and I know you can do it in your sleep."

Auden let out a breath. His routine difficulty. That was all Dorian wanted to talk about. He felt relief, though he couldn't help the worry that still pestered him, that Dorian might know the thoughts he'd been having lately.

Dorian squeezed his shoulder. "Olympic trials are less than two months away."

Auden's stomach clenched again but he forced himself to nod. He hated the feeling of dread, of doubt that clawed its way into his throat. Ever since World's, something had changed. There had always been pressure before, pressure to perform, to win, to be the best, but now, it felt like it was suffocating him every time anyone mentioned the Olympics or trials.

"Now is not the time to drop the ball," Dorian went on. "You're one of the top gymnasts here, and you've got a real shot at making it. Come by my office tomorrow and we'll start reworking your routines."

Auden nodded again, hoping to dislodge some of the worry heavy in his gut, glad when Dorian's attention was caught by Liam stepping out of bounds on his tuck. Moving over to the bench, he sank down next to Anya, eyeing the cold compress pressed to her shoulder.

"What was that?" she asked the moment Auden joined her. Removing the compress, she examined her shoulder. She was a slender girl with hair that fell to the middle of her back, and reminded Dorian of a Disney princess. Anya was lucky. She didn't have to worry about Olympic trials. With her shoulder injury, she was officially out of the running. It meant no training, no constant discussions of competitors, no weighing the stats against one another. When it came down to the trials, Auden would no longer be on a team. He'd be on his own.

He shook his head. "Just wanted to talk about the difficulty level." For a moment, he considered just telling Anya, telling her he wasn't excited about the trials, that the thought of them filled him with dread. He couldn't, though. She wouldn't understand. No one at the Elite Gymnastic Center would understand. They were all here for one purpose and it wasn't to avoid thinking about the Olympics.

Anya didn't acknowledge his words except to curse under her breath. "I'm late for physical therapy." She hopped off the bench and tossed Auden the compress. "We still going out tonight?"

"Yeah." He turned the compress over, the cold seeping into his hands. "Trayce is coming too."

Anya paused then smiled. "Did you invite him?"

Auden met her knowing gaze. "Does it matter?"

She shrugged. "You told him it wasn't hockey, right?"

"He's from Canada. That doesn't mean he's a stereotype." Actually, Auden had no idea if Trayce liked hockey or not. All he knew about Trayce's life in Canada was that he had lived with his parents in Toronto before they divorced and his mom had moved him to the States.

Anya didn't look impressed. "I gotta go. I'll see you and Trayce tonight."

As she left, Auden dropped the compress on the bench next to him. He couldn't wait to get out of the Center, even if just for the night, and the fact that he'd gotten Trayce to agree to come with him was something out of a fairytale. He couldn't help smiling as he gazed across the gym and his eyes fell on Trayce, pausing on the lines of his body, lean but well-built. Trayce hoisted himself up to the rings, arms straining, muscles quivering, but as he reached the holding height, he caught Auden's eye and flashed him a grin.

Tonight was going to be exactly what he needed to take his mind off training. It had been a hard year already, making it through World Championships and the mounting pressure of trials. Anything that took the edge off was worth it.

He watched Trayce drop to the ground, and stood from the bench. Just a few more hours of practice and he'd have a well-earned night out with his friends. He could definitely make it that far.

Technically, Auden hadn't invited Trayce to come out with him and Anya. He'd barely mentioned it the other night, right after Trayce had finished sucking him off. His mind hadn't been clear. The last thing he'd expected had been for Trayce to say it sounded like fun.

That might have been why, when Auden knocked on Trayce's door at quarter to eight, he wasn't surprised when Trayce answered wearing sweatpants and an old EGC tee shirt. Trayce pulled open the door and leaned against the frame, eyes grazing down Auden's body, smiling at his retro *The Who* shirt.

"I'm guessing you're not ready," Auden said after a minute. If Trayce's outfit was anything to go by, he didn't plan on being ready any time soon. Auden had spent too much time choosing between shirts already, making sure his plain brown hair looked something other than like he'd just rolled out of bed. When he did it, it looked stupid, but when Trayce did it, he looked completely fuckable. Life just wasn't fair.

Trayce blinked slowly, grey eyes flicking up to Auden's hazel ones. He tilted his head to the side. "I don't really feel like going out."

"Trayce." Auden had nothing to argue. He felt a small stab of disappointment, annoyance, but he paused at the look in Trayce's eye. He'd seen it before, several times since the first time Trayce had invited him back to his dorm, and instead of playing video games or watching TV, they'd ended up jerking each other off and then not speaking about it the next day. "I've been planning on this show for a month. I'm not missing it."

"So you'll miss the shitty opening act," Trayce said. "Nobody goes to see them anyway."

"That's all I'm worth to you?" Auden replied. "An opening-act's worth of sex?" He said it, but his eyes grazed down Trayce's chest, to the sliver of skin visible below the hem of the old tee-shirt, washed and dried too many times over the years.

Anya was always late anyway, he thought, standing in the dorm hallway, the walls painted an annoying shade of tan. And Trayce was exactly the kind of distraction he craved.

"Could be more." Trayce smirked, plucking at the hem of Auden's jacket as his gaze wandered further south.

Anya was waiting, but Trayce was right here, wearing that smile that made Auden want to do all sorts of things to his body. A few minutes of Anya's annoyance would be worth whatever Trayce had in store. Stepping forward, he pushed Trayce back into the room and stopped Trayce's grin with a kiss.

Auden's arms circled around Trayce's neck, pulling him closer as Trayce pressed him up against the door. He *was* going to miss the opening band, but he didn't care if it meant being here with Trayce. It was easy to make that choice, to follow the flicker of Trayce's gaze from his mouth to his eyes. Auden kissed him as they stumbled back from the door, shucking off his jacket in the process, only to land against a wall instead.

"There are better things to do than listen to out of tune drunk rock bands," Trayce murmured against his mouth, but Auden shut him up again, hands groping for Trayce's ass, hips surging against Trayce's. Talking wasn't why he was here.

Chapter 2
Punk Rock Boy

Auden breathed out at the press of Trayce's cock in his sweatpants, hard and rocking in against him. His own jeans would soon become too tight, too confining as Trayce moved against him, hips rolling into his. His hands moved to Trayce's waist, pushing at his shirt, sliding underneath, gliding over his toned muscles. *This* was why he was leaving Anya waiting downstairs. Any time he got Trayce under his hands, malleable to what he wanted, he'd take it.

Trayce licked up Auden's neck, a hand pressed flat against the door as he ground into Auden, a slow, torturous circle with his hips that left Auden breathless and flushed. This was exactly what he needed — a distraction, a moment when he could just relax and enjoy the feeling of being with Trayce. No one was talking about trials. There was nothing outside this room.

Auden met Trayce's mouth for a brief, mostly teeth and tongues, kiss, too busy panting for breath to do any more. He could feel Trayce's breath against his lower lip, feel the tip of his nose pressed to his.

"Shit," Trayce cursed as Auden pushed his hips up against him.

Auden wanted more, more than just Trayce against him. It was hot and sweaty and not enough, too much friction and not enough release, just pressure building. His boxers dragged against his throbbing cock with each twist of Trayce's hips, and he couldn't bite back the gasp that followed.

Trayce straddled Auden's thighs, their heights almost identical except by a centimeter or two. Their bodies undulated together, hips moving up and back, and Auden knew they had to stop before he came in his jeans.

"Trayce," he tried to say, but the word stuck in his throat, heat flooding his cheeks, mouth falling open to pant for breath. They usually got farther than this, but the pace was frantic now, hot breath panted against skin, pressure building in his cock with each rub, each twist.

Auden's fingers dug into Trayce's shoulder as he whined, muttering, "Fuck!" He wasn't going to make it past this, not with Trayce grinding against him, hot and hard, not slowing down in the least. It felt good, the tightening under his skin, knowing Trayce felt the same. When they were together like this, Auden could swear there was something else between them. It was in the way Trayce's hands gripped his waist and held him fast.

Trayce didn't stop, moving even faster now, and Auden could barely gasp for breath around the pressure in his cock. He was beginning to seriously regret putting on jeans, gasping and squeezing Trayce's shoulder.

He came before he could stop himself, overwhelmed by Trayce's body pressed against his, Trayce's hand grasping his side, pulling his hips in flush as they jerked and his head hit the door with a thunk.

"Shit," he muttered, shifting awkwardly against the mess in his jeans. He'd have to change before the concert.

Trayce smiled, moving his hand from the wall to Auden's jaw instead, tipping his chin back down. He kissed Auden without a word, slow and drawn-out, tongues sliding together as Auden kissed back, eyes closed. It was moments like this where he believed, almost believed, that this was more than just a fuck. He'd told himself enough times that he and Trayce were just friends, teammates, two guys who sometimes spent their evenings naked and sweaty together. Nothing more. And that had been fine, a few months ago, but a sense of normalcy was lacking in everything Auden did these days. Just once, he'd like to know what it felt like to be a normal twenty year old kid.

"My turn," Trayce murmured a moment later, stepping away from Auden and tugging him towards the bed by his shirt.

"I have to go," Auden said reluctantly, glancing at the alarm clock on Trayce's desk. A part of him didn't want to leave, not when there was the possibility of getting Trayce naked and on his back, vulnerable to him.

Trayce dropped his hand and shrugged. "If you *have* to. Or you could get over here and take your clothes off."

Auden couldn't suppress his smile as he shook his head. "Fuck you." He'd deal with Anya's annoyance at his lateness later. Right now, he had a smug Trayce to take care of. Stepping forward, he shoved Trayce's chest and Trayce fell backward onto the bed.

Trayce wasted no time, shedding his pants, kicking them away, and Auden climbed over him, straddling his legs and pausing as he looked down. Trayce pulled off his shirt, revealing his perfect gymnast body, meeting Auden's eyes, a grin playing at his mouth. As much as Auden saw the same muscles and expanses of bare skin every day, it was always better when it was Trayce, when they were alone.

"Good choice," Trayce murmured as Auden's hand slid down his chest.

It had been months since they'd started this and not much had changed. Trayce was just as adamant now as he was then about this arrangement only concerning sex. What was the point of romance? he had asked.

Their lips met for a short kiss, hardly anything, but Auden went back for another, biting at Trayce's bottom lip, sucking until Trayce's hand slid to the back of his neck, stroking the short hair. Auden felt Trayce's cock pressed against his, completely hard.

"Mmm," Trayce hummed into the kiss as Auden straddled him on the bed, hips pressing down. Anything was worth it to get Trayce like this, his breath coming shorter when Auden pulled back, lips sliding down his chest.

He made sure to take his time, tongue sliding over Trayce's skin, down his sternum, licking and sucking. He left marks despite Trayce's sharp breath, a wordless reminder to be careful. Anything they had to explain to the coaches wasn't welcome. He'd never left a visible mark above Trayce's collar, though he'd considered it once or twice. He thought about it now, but Trayce's hand was in his hair, urging him down, past his hip bones to where his cock stood ready and eager.

He glanced up as he reached Trayce's prick, hard and hot, heavy in his hand as he slid it down, gripping the base and pulling gently. He loved the idea that he could make Trayce bite his lip and strain against him, that Trayce wanted this as much as he did.

Trayce let out a slow breath as Auden slid his tongue past Trayce's hip bone, teeth scraping against the skin. He shifted on his knees, pressing kisses down Trayce's stomach until he reached his cock, then licking up the length.

This was what normal kids did, Auden thought as he stroked Trayce's prick, weighing the heaviness against his palm. They slept around. They fucked in bathrooms of sleazy bars they were too young to get into. This was as close to normal as Auden was going to get. Still, there were other kinds of normal, like relationships and dinners and waking up next to each other.

Trayce never said a word, only huffing out a breath every once in a while, his hand carding through Auden's hair as Auden leaned down and took him in.

Sucking cock wasn't something Auden had ever thought he would pride himself on, but the way Trayce's breathing increased, the way he pushed his cock up into his mouth, was proof enough of his skill.

He used his hand to jerk Trayce off along with each slide of his mouth, each flick of his tongue when he pulled back, licking the head and listening for the change in breath that usually accompanied it. Moving back in, he sucked harder, more determined to get Trayce off, to make it as good as possible. He wanted Trayce to want it as badly as he did, to admit it wasn't just fucking.

"Come on," Trayce muttered, impatient, but he stretched back as Auden licked the length of his cock, hand working with his mouth.

Auden didn't need the sharp gasp to warn him, seconds before Trayce came. He didn't need the hand tightening in his hair as he pulled back, stroking out Trayce's release, come decorating the comforter. He pulled his sticky hand away and reached for Trayce's discarded boxers on the floor, wiping away the mess.

"Ah, fuck," Trayce breathed finally, spread out on the bed. Auden sat beside him. He shifted against the uncomfortable wetness in his jeans. "That was good."

Auden glanced over but Trayce had his arms thrown over his face. If Trayce asked him to stay, to skip the concert, he would.

Just as he thought it, his phone vibrated in his pocket. He knew without even looking that it was Anya. Trayce must have heard it because he made a noise. "Your girlfriend is waiting."

Auden pulled out the phone and sent a quick response to her impatient message.

"Maybe because I'm late," he pointed out, rolling off the bed.

Trayce shrugged. "This is better than going out. Besides, early practice tomorrow. Dorian will murder you if you're not in tip-top shape."

"I should go," Auden said simply. He didn't want to think about practice or what Dorian would do if he showed up tired tomorrow.

"Enjoy your concert," Trayce said, waving him away from the bed. "Maybe you'll meet someone nice." It was laced with sarcasm and amusement. "Someone who'll bring you flowers and light candles during sex."

"Fuck you," Auden muttered, reaching for the doorknob. Just because Trayce would never do that didn't mean there weren't people who would. Just because Trayce never asked him to stay, it didn't mean someone else wouldn't.

"Aw, don't leave mad," Trayce said, pushing himself up and grinning at Auden. "You know what they say—you're never supposed to go to bed angry."

Auden yanked open the door. "You're a jerk."

"Let's not get sentimental," Trayce drawled, but Auden left before he could go on. Shutting the door with a snap behind him, he headed back to his room to change. It wasn't that he didn't know full well what Trayce was like; he simply hoped, sometimes, that he'd prove him wrong.

"I know, I know," Auden said at Anya's crossed arms and impatient look as he slid into her piece of junk car, a 2015 Ford Focus—once white but now a rusty brown—with a missing side mirror. Auden wasn't sure it should even run considering how old it was. Anya stared at Auden as he buckled his seatbelt, and he turned to her, frowning at her gaze. "I'm sorry, okay?"

"I guess Trayce isn't coming?" she said, less of a question and more of a disapproving huff.

"No." He sighed. They really needed to get going. The sun had already set, leaving the desert landscape of Phoenix glowing orange from streetlamps instead. Auden really didn't need a jacket considering the high temperature had been ninety-two and it was barely seventy-eight now that the sun had gone down, but it was his only excuse to wear something other than tank tops and sweatpants.

"So you just let me wait while you fuck your pseudo-boyfriend?" Anya tossed him a displeased look as they pulled away from the Center. The parking lot was meticulously landscaped with Joshua trees and a flowering Palo Verde in the center divider. The flowers had already begun to fall, the typical spring shower of yellow petals that covered the dark pavement.

Auden frowned out the window. "I didn't mean to. It's just, when we're alone, it's like he's... Never mind." It was stupid, but when it was just him and Trayce, he couldn't help himself. He wanted to touch him, to kiss him, and Trayce wanted it too. Trayce may have said it was just getting off, a way to take the edge off, but Trayce had never turned him down.

Wishful thinking, that's what that was, Auden told himself firmly.

The Center was fairly new to the valley, only about eight years old. Following the example of the World Olympics Gymnastic Academy in Texas, the directors had gone after former Olympians for coaches, including Dorian Stuart, one of the best coaches in the country. Auden knew he was lucky to be coached by Dorian, a former Olympic gold medalist. Gymnasts would kill for Dorian's experience. As it was, though, Auden wasn't sure it even mattered at this point.

The Center was set-up as much like any university Auden had ever seen, with buildings separated by winding cement paths, cacti sprouting up between tan-colored buildings. Though the sky was dark now, the lights of Phoenix blocking out any stars, during the day, it was perpetually blue with hardly a cloud to be seen.

Anya shook her head as she pulled out of the large parking lot and onto the street. The Center was a large area just outside of Ahwatukee in the shadow of the mountain, though Auden would have said it was more of a large hill. As far as he'd seen, there were no real mountains in Arizona. His dad had called it a pile of dirt when he'd come down to see the Center two years ago.

Most of the area around the Center was new construction: clean, painted cement to match the desert sand and carefully landscaped cacti and mesquite trees. Showers of tiny yellow flowers skittered across the windshield of the car as they drove.

"I know what you want to happen with Trayce," Anya said as they merged onto the freeway, and she cut off a truck in the process. "But fucking around isn't going to help."

Auden pressed his forehead against the window. "I'm really not in the mood for this lecture."

"How about I lecture you on punctuality?"

Auden felt a twinge of guilt in his stomach. "I'm sorry I was late."

"Was it at least worth it?"

"Well, the sex was good, if that's what you mean."

Anya rolled her eyes. "Better have been to stand me up. And Trayce is still refusing to admit you're boyfriends?"

"Trayce and I are just friends," Auden said simply. Boyfriends was a word that would probably make Trayce grimace.

"Friends, yes, I've heard that before," she said, shooting him a look. "Friends with benefits. Have you never watched a movie or reality television? It never works out. Besides, Olympics trials are two months away."

"So?" He was starting to get really tired of hearing about them.

She frowned at him and veered across two lanes of traffic for the exit to Tempe. "So the last thing you want now is a distraction."

"Trayce is not a distraction. He's just..."

"Something to do?"

Auden couldn't explain Trayce to Anya. She'd just argue that he was using Trayce as an excuse not to find someone else who actually liked him. In a way, she was right. Trayce was something to do, something that shouldn't distract him from training, from Olympic trials. It was an easy out. Of course, that didn't account for the way Auden felt when Trayce smiled at him sometimes, like he might actually care.

Sitting back in his seat, Auden sighed. "You've got it so easy," he said instead. "You don't even have to worry about trials."

Anya laughed shortly, pausing at a stop light. They were already downtown, surrounded by bright shop lights, bars and clubs. College students filled the sidewalks, and Auden gazed out at them. They were people with no concerns. They spent all their nights drinking and partying and not thinking about their futures, not like Auden did every single day.

"Yeah, I don't have to worry about trials because I tore my rotator cuff which means all my training goes to shit and I miss an Olympic year and now I have to wait four more years before I'll even have another chance." She sighed bitterly. "I'm so lucky."

Auden didn't reply. Every time anyone mentioned the trials, which was every day, he began to feel more and more dread. He wasn't sure why—he should have been excited. He should have been fantasizing about making the Olympic team and traveling to France. Instead, he'd rather not think about it at all.

In all the time he'd been training as a gymnast, the Olympics had always been there, somewhere in the future. Unreachable. Fifteen years of scrapes and bruises, pulled muscles and painful falls, of his dad counting every penny that went into training, he couldn't just let whatever feeling of dread that came up every time he so much as heard the word "trials" run him out of something he'd worked so hard for.

Anya glanced at him as they passed under an orange streetlamp. "You're not going to let Trayce get in the way of the Olympics, right? Because I'm counting on you. You have to make it for all the rest of us."

The last thing to get in the way of the Olympics would be a guy, Auden admitted. She was right, though. There were people counting on him; her, Dorian, his parents. His future depended on how he performed in the next few months.

As they drove, Auden swallowed back his reluctance and shook his head at Anya. "Of course not. I'm gonna make the team." He needed to put whatever this was, this unease, behind him. He'd come too far to give up now.

"You're definitely gonna make it." Anya smiled back and they pulled into a dim parking lot a minute later.

She was right. His whole childhood had been dedicated to one thing, and giving up now would be throwing away everything he'd worked for. He'd just have to work harder. And he would.

"Why do we have to park so far away?" Auden asked as they got out. The lot was dark except for a sole lamp at the far end. Auden was fairly sure this was where people went to get mugged.

"Because I'm not paying ten bucks to park on the same piece of cement five blocks from here."

Sometimes it was difficult to believe they lived in the desert when all Auden could see was buildings, freeways, and shopping centers. The only things close to nature were the transplanted Saguaro cacti, the palm trees in boxes, prickly shrubs on the side of the road. It wasn't like San Diego where his parents and younger sister lived. There, everything was green and lush, fed with constant sprinkler systems.

The place they were going was less of a concert venue and more of a bar that sometimes featured local artists. The doorman barely even glanced at their fake IDs as they entered. Auden only had one to get in to see the bands. Drinking was strictly forbidden when it came to training. Dorian was all about the nutrition rules.

Inside, it was already crowded. The stage was empty, though. Whoever had been on before had already packed up. Auden couldn't care less about opening acts. He was there to see Barefoot Matador, a punk band from Tucson. They weren't exactly famous, but Auden liked their music. It was a nice change from the Center where the lights went out at ten on the nose every night and any music played after that had to be done through headphones. Anyone he played Matador's music to usually asked why he liked punk.

He couldn't always explain it, but it was such a change from what he'd grown up with—there was an especially traumatic memory of middle school dances and being laughed at by all the popular girls as Uptown Funk played in the background. He'd decided right then that pop music was not his scene.

The same group of girls who seemed to follow the band around was already grouped around the stage. Most of the rest of the people in the bar were busy drinking and standing around for the show.

"You want something to drink?" Auden asked over the piped in music playing above them.

"Water," she said and moved away to stake out a spot close enough to the stage to get a good view but no so close they'd be stuck in a mosh. Explaining strange bruises to coaches was not an easy thing to do and Auden figured it was best to avoid questions.

At the bar, Auden waited for the bartender to finish with a group at the other end.

"Buy you a beer?"

Auden was surprised at the offer, and he answered before he even glanced over. "I don't drink." He almost changed his mind, though, when he turned to the guy who had slid up next to him. He was a little taller than him with shaggy black hair, dark stubble on his jaw, and though he wasn't particularly well-muscled, he wasn't a stick.

"Soda then?" the guy asked, a smile curving the corner of his mouth.

Auden wasn't used to being hit on in bars, especially by guys who were ten times hotter than anyone he knew, except perhaps Trayce.

"I can't have caffeine," he said, though, cursing the diet charts pinned up all around the gym.

"Aren't you going for godliness," the guy said, grinning. "Water, then. You can't say no to that." Auden smiled slightly as the guy gestured for the bartender. "Bottle of water for my friend."

"Sure, Shane," the bartender replied.

Auden paused. "You must come here a lot." The guy arched an eyebrow and Auden nodded at the bartender. "Bartender knows your name."

Shane nodded. "This place is like my second home. They give me stage time and I give them money for beer."

"You're a musician?" There wasn't anything about him to suggest it aside from his unkempt hair and the calluses on his fingers that Auden noticed as Shane took the beer the bartender brought him along with the bottle of water.

"I take it you missed my set." Shane took a drink and smiled as Auden paused. "It's cool. I'm not the main attraction. Yet." He paused, taking in Auden. "You've got some guns on you."

"They're not as big as—I mean, thanks," he said, stopping himself halfway through saying they weren't as big as some of the guys' on his team. As far as gymnast bodies went, his was fairly average in muscle size.

"Is that why you don't drink? A workout addict?"

Auden laughed. If only that was it. If he just liked working out, he wouldn't feel so pressured all the time.

"I wish," he said before he could stop himself then bit his tongue. "I mean, I'm a gymnast."

"That's cool. I do a lot of hiking, rock climbing. I bet you'd really like it. It can definitely get your blood pumping." He grinned at Auden but a sound from the stage caught his attention. The band had finished setting up and was taking their places. Shane glanced at Auden and then grabbed a napkin. He took a pen out of his pocket and scribbled something down. "Show's starting. You should call me some time."

Auden took the napkin he handed over and didn't say anything for a second, not until Shane's back was turned.

"I don't really have time for anything but gymnastics."

Shane glanced back, eyes grazing down his body. "What's your name?"

"Auden."

"Well, Auden, you might say that, but you're here, aren't you?" He smirked and disappeared into the crowd.

Standing at the bar, Auden stared at the number. It was the first one anyone had ever given him. Shaking himself, he stuffed it into his pocket and pushed his way through the crowd to where Anya waited.

"What took you so long?" she asked as he handed over the water.

Auden shook his head but didn't answer her, turning to watch the band. His mind lingered over Shane, though, and he couldn't say he paid much attention to the show that night.

Chapter 3
Changing Elements

Auden felt the strain in his arms as he lifted the ten pound weights, a repetition of twenty and then a short rest period. Warm-ups always seemed to take the most time. Auden watched some of the younger kids tumbling on the other side as Dorian looked on, arms crossed and a serious expression on his face. If it hadn't been for Jules, Auden would have thought that Dorian only had one expression.

As he watched, Jules stepped up behind Dorian, poking him in the back and making him jump. Auden smiled to himself, watching them from across the gym. Dorian and Jules were the stuff of legend — if not from their days in the Olympics then from their relationship that seemed to fluctuate like a suspension bridge in the wind.

"Disgusting isn't it? Love," Trayce said from behind Auden. "Don't know why people put themselves through it."

Auden turned away from Dorian and Jules as Trayce grabbed a weight. "Not everyone is emotionally stunted."

Trayce laughed. "Everyone is emotionally stunted. Some people just show it less. How was the show last night?"

"It was fine," Auden muttered. He'd put the napkin with Shane's number on it on his nightstand but hadn't called yet. He wanted to, really wanted to, but what would he say? He'd never been on a real date. What he and Trayce did could barely be considered a relationship. They were friends only because they were on the same team and Trayce was the only one who understood the rules of the Masters of the X video game. Whenever Auden tried to play with Anya, she said shooting people and looking for a secret chest was too boring. No matter that finding the chest meant winning and completing a twenty-level game. Auden had been stuck at level seven for the past month — the next level had to be secret. That was why he couldn't find it.

"I thought you liked shitty punk bands." Trayce grinned at Auden's unimpressed look.

Punk wasn't just screaming into microphones and jumping into crowds. It was an escape. He didn't have to think about it. He could just listen and pretend he was in the middle of a mosh pit where nothing mattered except the push and shove of the music.

Trayce might not have understood, but it was a release for Auden. He didn't need to understand all the words or learn to play the chords on a guitar. It wasn't like gymnastics — there was less structure, more freedom. He could close his eyes and get lost in the music. Everything else just melted away.

"It isn't shitty."

"It's no Beatles."

Auden rolled his eyes. "Forgive me if I don't trust a Canadian's judgment of music."

"Fucker," Trayce said good-naturedly. "I may be Canadian by birth, but I haven't lived there since I was thirteen."

"Seven years isn't enough to wipe out a lifetime of bad music. What is Nickleback on, their twentieth album, and they still suck?" He glanced at Trayce as he did his reps of weights. If he called Shane, what would that mean for him and Trayce? He was perfectly aware of Trayce's stance on love, but as much as Auden tried to tell himself that what he and Trayce did didn't matter, he knew he was just lying to himself. He looked forward to their moments alone, when Trayce would invite him to his dorm after practice. Shane would change that. He paused. "At the trials, are you going to be trying out for the US team or the Canadian team?"

He hadn't really thought about what Trayce would do. He knew he sometimes got a lot of shit for coming down here to train instead of staying in Canada. Trayce maintained that the US had better coaches and better facilities. Auden thought he liked the weather better too.

"I was thinking I'd just wait a couple years and try out for the hockey team instead. Much more Canadian," Trayce replied, deadpan. "Shit, Auden. I applied for citizenship last year. You really think I'm going to abandon my team?"

"Well, you are from Canada."

"And Danell Leyva was from Cuba, but he competed on the US team."

He had a point, and Auden would admit to feeling relieved. The possibility of Trayce ditching him for Canada gave him an unexpected lurch in his stomach. Not that it mattered what Trayce did, Auden told himself. In the trials, they would be on their own. No more teams. That's what all the work was for.

"I guess," Auden agreed finally, and Trayce smiled. It was the kind of smile that made Auden want to throw away Shane's number and convince himself that Trayce felt something more than friendship for him.

"I'm not gonna abandon you just like that," Trayce said, grabbing him by the neck and giving him a slight shake. "I need you to make the team."

Auden stared at him for a second, wondering what exactly he meant. A balloon began to expand in his chest, pressing against his heart as he thought of how much trials meant to everyone else. Trayce wanted this so badly he'd do anything to get it. And he wanted Auden to get it too.

"Yeah?" Auden asked, his skin tingling where Trayce's hand still rested.

Trayce grinned after a second. "I gotta at least have some competition."

Auden rolled his eyes as Trayce dropped his hand, the hopeful bubble bursting. "I'm sure everyone who makes the team will be good enough."

Trayce smirked. "Maybe, but it's also in France this year. That means all that romantic stuff you love."

"Right," Auden scoffed. "Because you'd definitely –"

"Auden!" Dorian interrupted him. He'd left the younger kids and gestured at Auden. "Let's go to my office and work out your routines."

Auden left Trayce without another word and followed Dorian out of the gym. They walked down the hallways plastered with photographs of past winners—championship winners, Olympic team members. The last photo they passed was of him, his World Champion gold medal on the pommel horse. That moment seemed so long ago even though it had barely been a few months. That had been the moment everything had become real.

Dorian led the way into his office. Auden had only been in it once before, though he remembered little of the visit. It had merely been a formality after deciding to come to train at the Center, just his parents signing papers since he hadn't been eighteen yet. Now, at twenty, it seemed like a whole lifetime had passed since then.

Dorian's office was scattered with papers, and filing cabinets stood against the wall. Photographs hung up here as well—photos of Dorian's Olympics, gold and silver medals, even a picture of Jules receiving his gold medal in the all-around in 2012. Dorian took his seat and waited for Auden to do the same.

Whatever changes Dorian suggested, Auden would make them. He wasn't a quitter—he couldn't be.

Dorian leaned back in his chair and smiled at Auden. It was a rare thing to see. "I've been coaching for more than ten years now, and of all the people I've seen come through here, I don't think I've seen anyone with as much potential as you."

An invisible boulder settled on Auden's chest as he sat there, heavy and suffocating.

"When you won gold in World's, I knew then we'd have to work harder than ever. The Olympics are not just going to be handed to you. You have to want it, and you have to be talented enough to get it. There are hundreds of other gymnasts out there who have dreamed of the moment they'll be chosen for an Olympic team. Hell, there are gymnasts in that gym back there who are thinking the same thing right at this very moment. Most of them won't ever make it. You have a chance that they'll only dream of. If you want to win, you have to be willing to sacrifice everything else for the next two months. You have to push harder, want it more, be better." Dorian paused, leaning back in his chair.

Auden knew all of this—he'd heard it before, but somehow, it all seemed so much more serious now, as if one mistake could jeopardize everything. He was going to get through it, for Dorian, for

Anya.

Dorian smiled then, surprising Auden, not reassuring him at all though it was supposed to.

"So let's talk about your routines. I think all we need are just a few new elements here and there and you'll be Olympics material."

Gathering himself together, Auden took a deep breath around the invisible hand squeezing his throat and sat up straighter. He wasn't going to quit. He wouldn't just throw it away for the sinking feeling in his stomach. Instead, he tried his best to listen to what Dorian said and promised to work hard on incorporating the new elements into his routine. He'd do whatever it took.

Dinner was three ounces of chicken, a salad, and an orange. Auden slid into the seat next to Anya, setting his plate down on the table. Anya barely glanced at him, too intent on watching someone on the other side of the room.

"Do you think Liam is straight?"

"Probably." Auden didn't know, but he could guess. Most of his conversations with Liam tended to be about leverage and upper body strength. Then again, that was how most of his conversations went with the other guys at EGC. The only one he ever talked to about anything else was...

Trayce plopped down in the chair on the opposite side of the table, rattling Auden's plate as he sat down.

"Hey," Anya greeted him, still gazing over at Liam a few tables over. Auden rolled his eyes at her and poked at his salad instead.

"Hey," Trayce replied, nodding at Auden. "So how many elements did Dorian add?"

"Just two and changed two others." Dorian had been right about the routine. Playing it safe was for rookies, and he'd been at this long enough to know his limits and where to push them. The difficulty didn't bother him; he could do the new elements fairly easily. They hadn't been anything crazy like new dismounts.

"Ugh, I'm so jealous," Anya huffed, pushing the salad around her plate. "Paris. You get to go to Paris."

"I haven't made the team," Auden reminded her.

"Please," she scoffed, waving an inconsequential hand, "you will, and then you'll be going off to Paris without me." She sighed, sounding forlorn. "Do you think I'd fit in your suitcase? I'm small and flexible!"

Thinking about Paris wasn't nearly as exciting as it should have been, and Auden shrugged at her question. "Sure. You can keep me company as I watch from the sidelines."

Trayce shot him a look over his water bottle. "Dorian's already picked out your seat on the plane."

If Auden didn't know Trayce any better, he would have said Trayce was jealous over Dorian's treatment. Glancing up, he caught Trayce's eyes, grey with flecks of blue. He looked away from Trayce licking his lips slowly.

"He's got yours picked out too."

"You've always been his favorite," Trayce went on, nudging Auden's ankle under the table.

"Can we just talk about something else?" he said instead. Sometimes, it felt like there was nothing else to talk about.

For his question, he received an arched eyebrow from Trayce. Anya was busy staring across the cafeteria, trying to get a good look at Liam where he sat with the rest of their teammates.

"If you're worried you're not gonna make it," Trayce said, lowering his voice slightly and leaning over the table towards Auden, something more sincere than Auden had seen before in his eyes.

"No," he interrupted Trayce. "I mean. I just want to talk about something else."

Trayce didn't reply, leaning back and watching Auden instead. His gaze made Auden uncomfortable in a different kind of way, like he could see right through his fake confidence.

"Trayce, do you think Liam's straight?" Anya asked instead, thankfully changing the subject, although not to one Auden was particularly interested in either.

"As an arrow," Trayce replied with such certainty that it made Auden glance at him. Trayce smirked back and stabbed his salad.

Back in his dorm, Auden flopped down on the entirely too small twin bed that came standard in the Center and sighed at the ceiling. Just once he'd like to get through a meal without someone bringing up trials or training or competition stats. Glancing around his walls, it just made his stomach sink. The walls were covered with pictures of old Olympic medalists. Each one had a medal hanging around his neck and grinned at the camera as though it was the best day of his life. He hadn't changed his walls in the past couple years since coming to the Center, and when he'd put those up, he'd been so sure he'd be one of them soon. Now, looking at them just made him feel sick to his stomach.

Groaning, Auden threw an arm over his face. Why couldn't things go back to how they had been before the World Championships? The Olympics had been so far off at that point. They had been an untouchable dream, something that might never come to pass. Now, they were real, tangible, less than two months away, and he'd endured nothing but endless confidence from everyone he knew that he would make the team. It was enough to make him hate the idea of going. What if he didn't make it?

There hadn't been so much pressure then. There hadn't been this pit of dread in his stomach. There had to be something to make it go away, something to distract him from the impending competition, the fate of his career as a gymnast.

As he lay there, Dorian's words came back to him, as they so often had since the World Championships; "*A medal at World's paves the way to the Olympics... I expect to see you on that team come July.*" He'd played them over and over. When he'd said it, back in December, Auden hadn't thought anything of it. It had been exactly what he wanted, but it had sunk into his consciousness over the past few months. It had become a huge expectation, one he was required to live up to.

He didn't even know when the excitement had turned to lead in his stomach. Everything had gotten more serious, more focused, and he felt like he hadn't fallen in line somehow. Everyone had upped their expectations and somehow, things had changed.

For a moment, he contemplated walking down to Trayce's dorm. Trayce would be there—the only other thing to do on a Wednesday night was hang out in the lounge and watch TV. He knew how it would go; he and Trayce would start out playing Masters of the X but they wouldn't make it past one round before they'd end up tangled in Trayce's bed. They both knew the video game was just a pretense. It wouldn't help him at all.

That was one option, Auden thought as he lay on his bed, listening to the thud of music coming through the walls from a neighboring room. He'd done it before, but there was always something missing. No matter what he told Anya, he was well-aware of his unrealistic crush on Trayce, Trayce, who didn't feel remotely the same.

What else was there to do but sit there and worry himself with thoughts of Olympic trials, though? Sitting up, Auden resolved that even if it wasn't anything to Trayce, it was still something to do. He reached for his dorm key on his bedside table, but his eyes fell on the crumpled napkin with Shane's phone number on it. It had been a few days since the show, and Auden had never been very good at taking the first step with guys, but what did he really have to lose?

Grabbing his cell out of his pocket, he tapped in Shane's number and waited.

"Shane's phone," came the answer a moment later.

"Hi," Auden said, grimacing at the word, so plain. "It's Auden, from the Barefoot Matador show?" He wasn't sure why he said it like a question, but maybe Shane wouldn't remember him. Maybe he gave his number to lots of guys at bars.

"The gymnast," Shane supplied a second later, a grin in his voice. "Was beginning to think you wouldn't call."

Auden swung his legs off the side of his bed and scooted to the edge. "I told you I didn't have time for anything but training."

"Usually that's a polite brush-off," Shane said. "Didn't know you were serious." There was a slight pause. "So if you're so busy, what made you change your mind?"

"I didn't change my mind." Auden shifted, glancing up at the photograph of the 2008 Olympics with both Dorian and Jules in the middle of the team photo. He didn't even remember watching that year—he'd only been four years old—but he'd watched it enough times afterward to remember every detail. His mother liked to say that it had been the beginning of the end. "I was just thinking that it'd be nice to get out."

"Out?" Shane repeated curiously.

Auden wasn't sure how to put it. He just needed to be somewhere other than the gym all the time. He needed to be around someone who didn't constantly talk about body mass and muscle strength.

"I train more than thirty hours a week. It's almost a full-time job these days. It can get... tiring, and if you were still interested, I thought maybe we could hang out." He wasn't sure he was quite getting his point across. He wasn't sure he could just come out and say that Shane was very good-looking and would he want to climb a mountain and make out at the top? "You said you hiked?"

There was another pause in which something knotted up inside Auden's chest and he was reminded why he didn't try this with anyone other than Trayce who would agree with the simple promise of getting inside Auden's pants.

"I do," Shane agreed at length. "In fact, I was planning on going this weekend. You sure you want to try, though? It's a bit rougher than jumping around on a mat."

Auden laughed. "You have no idea how many times I've been injured on a mat. I'm sure I can handle hiking."

"Okay," Shane agreed after a second, the smile back in his voice, and it made Auden excited just to hear it. "How about you meet me at the Echo Canyon trailhead at Camelback Mountain Saturday morning, bright and early."

Auden couldn't believe he was doing this. He'd have to skip practice, and Dorian was super strict about any outside sports, but this could be his only chance—Dorian would kill him if he found out. "Yeah." Besides, his heart fluttered stupidly when Shane laughed on the other end of the phone.

"I'll see you then, gymnast."

Auden hung up, a grin spreading across his face. He'd just made a date with someone outside of the Center. That was definitely a first.

He tried not to think of what Dorian would say when he missed practice, but it was only a supplementary practice. Surely, it wasn't that big of a deal? Though he thought it, he knew it wasn't true.

He wasn't going to let apprehension about training get in the way of the elation filling him as he sat there. Flopping back on his bed, he realized he was actually looking forward to tomorrow because tomorrow was one day closer to Saturday.

Chapter 4

Up the Mountain

Somehow, Auden talked Anya into letting him borrow her car and followed his phone's directions to Camelback Mountain. It had been years since he'd been hiking—he couldn't even remember the last time—but he made sure to bring plenty of water and sunscreen. His body was a jangle of nerves as he navigated the freeways and found his way to the trailhead. If he thought about it, this was his first real date.

He couldn't count what he did with Trayce as dating. They never went out anywhere; Trayce never kissed him outside the bedroom; they never held hands or did whatever else people did on dates. Auden was embarrassed to say his only dating references came from pop culture and too many chick flicks that Anya made him watch—okay, so he not-so-secretly liked them. Either way, his only references came from movies and TV which couldn't be good.

Shane was waiting for him when he pulled up, just as good-looking as Auden remembered, although the only time he'd seen him had been in a half-dark bar where anyone was bound to look good. Shane did, though, with a messy curl falling over his forehead. He grinned at Auden as he stepped out of the car into the bright sunlight. Despite being early, it was already warm outside and it would only get hotter as the day went on.

The mountain loomed before them, sandy soil peppered with dull green desert plants. Overhead, the sky shone a clear, bright blue with not a single cloud. A warm breeze picked up as Auden stepped towards Shane.

"I see you escaped the gym," Shane said, tossing a backpack

over his shoulder and grinning at Auden.

"I get days off," he said, trying not to let the nerves take over as he spoke. He didn't mention that Saturdays were usually extra practice hours outside normal training. Trayce would be there today along with the others going for the trials. Dorian kept saying they needed all the practice they could get and Auden skipping one was sure to get him in trouble. That was not what he wanted to think about today, not when he was on a date — a real date — with someone who wasn't Trayce, not that he and Trayce had ever gone on a date. Trayce would probably have laughed if he'd ever suggested it.

Stop thinking about Trayce, he told himself firmly as he followed Shane to the trailhead.

"And you want to spend your time off climbing a mountain?" Shane grinned back at him, and Auden felt an unfamiliar flutter in his stomach.

"It's either that or watch cartoons all morning. I'm sure the company is infinitely better here."

Shane laughed, easy and open. "You assume correctly. We should get started before it gets too hot."

It seemed easy for Shane to make conversation, but Auden cast around for something to say as they started up the mountain, through rocky terrain and spiky bushes. The only things that came to mind, however, were about training and gymnastics, and all the things he didn't want to think about today, not on a date with a hot musician who looked especially good in his shorts as he climbed over rocks. He couldn't help admiring the view, but he jumped as Shane glanced back.

"You do this a lot?" Auden asked as they came to a steep portion and Shane went up first. Shane held out a hand to help Auden. As Auden took it, he felt the warmth of Shane's palm, fingers gripping his hand and pulling him up. It felt so different than anyone else, but maybe it was just the newness of the situation that made him feel jumbled up and nervous at everything that happened.

The sun beat down from above, a blinding light that made everything on the trail look washed out, aloe plants' spiky leaves drooping towards the ground. Auden gave the disjointed limbs of the jumping cholla cactus a wide berth, avoiding the spiky balls that had fallen on the ground. They had a tendency to lodge in people's legs no matter how much you avoided them.

"All the time. Don't tell me you're one of those people who think Phoenix is just tanning and swimming pools and air conditioned malls?"

"Uh," Auden hesitated. Phoenix certainly wasn't like home in San Diego with the beach and nice, temperate weather all the time. "I don't really have a lot of time to even go to malls."

Shane smiled. "There's a lot more to it. You should get out more."

"And do what?" Auden asked skeptically, scrambling up the loose gravel on the path.

Shane shrugged. "Lots of stuff. There's hiking, rock climbing, air balloons, tubing down the Salt River. You ever been?"

Auden shook his head. For all the time he'd spent living there, the most he'd ever done was wander down Mill Avenue on a Friday night with the kids from the University.

"You should come some time," Shane said, releasing Auden's hand as they got up the slope. Auden's palm tingled where they'd touched. "I bet you look really good in swim trunks."

Auden smiled, though he felt his face heating up, and not from the climb. Even if it was his first real date, it wasn't the first time he'd been around someone he liked. He wasn't like this with Trayce, but he knew Trayce better. They were friends. He and Shane... well, they definitely weren't friends yet.

It felt good to be outside, away from the gym, somewhere he could breathe without someone asking about his plans—less asking and more telling him how great the Olympics were going to be. At least Shane didn't do that. Shane didn't mention anything about gymnastics as they hiked up, passing a few people going the opposite direction.

It was a strenuous hike, and Shane glanced back a few times to make sure Auden hadn't fallen behind. Sweat began to soak his clothes, the temperature rising with the sun. What breeze there had been at the foot of the mountain was long gone.

"Doing okay?" Shane asked, a smirk at the corner of his lips.

"Fine," Auden replied. "No worse than a regular workout except I don't have to worry about breaking my ankle every time I step down." He grimaced to himself as he said it—he couldn't even go one morning without bringing up training.

Luckily, Shane laughed. "Most people I bring up here collapse after the first ten minutes."

"I'm not most people." Auden did have to admit that if he hadn't had so much training, it would have been a painful climb, but as it was, he could enjoy the view in front of him as Shane walked.

"Yeah, you're not," Shane said after a second, catching his eye and nodding towards the path. "We're almost there. One last push."

Auden smiled to himself and fell into step beside Shane as they pushed up the mountain to the top.

"You seriously do this?" Auden asked as Shane settled on top of the big rock, a thin blanket spread out beneath him.

Shane grinned. "It's relaxing. Trust me."

Auden eyed the rock again. It was a large, wide rock with a semi-flattened top, but it wasn't the rock that made him nervous. It was what could be living underneath it. Just because he didn't go out didn't mean he didn't know what lived amongst the cholla and yucca plants. There were all sorts of things he never wanted to encounter—scorpions, tarantulas, rattlesnakes—and yet Shane looked completely comfortable sitting cross-legged on this rock.

"If I get bit by something..." Auden said, moving carefully over to the rock and sitting down.

"Then I will take you to the hospital," Shane promised dutifully. "Just sit there and relax. The whole point of meditation is finding peace within yourself."

Auden wasn't sure he was really meditating kind of person, but he wanted to try it, if only because Shane asked him to. It couldn't be that bad.

"So you climb all the way up here to meditate?" he asked, trying to keep the skepticism out of his words, but it leaked through anyway.

Shane shrugged, taking Auden's hand and holding it between

his as he closed his eyes and breathed in deeply. Auden didn't think he could concentrate that well, not with Shane touching him like that. "Sometimes it helps for writing music. Sometimes I just need to get away from everything." He cracked his eyes open and met Auden's unsure gaze. "I think you'd get a lot out of it."

"Are you saying I'm not relaxed?"

Shane still hadn't released Auden's hand, and he stroked his fingers down the back of it. Despite the sun beating down, Auden shivered.

"I know I can be distracting, but you've been distracted all morning."

"I'm just thinking about training," Auden admitted. "Which I don't want to think about—"

"So don't," Shane interrupted. "You know why I came up to you that night at the bar?"

"Because I have a well-toned physique?" Auden smiled at Shane. It was no secret that was why people noticed him. It was why anyone noticed a gymnast—his body was a mark of pride, something he'd worked for to get what he wanted.

Shane tried not to smile, shaking his head, but Auden could see it tugging the corners of his mouth. "I'll be honest and say yes, but you looked like you needed some fun. All that training is stressful, and for what?"

"For the Olympics," Auden replied, confused for a second. It was the only answer he'd had for years. He'd spent the last ten years focused on one goal.

Shane shrugged. "Just doesn't seem worth it to me." He released Auden's hand finally and patted his knee instead. "So how about we get rid of all that stress?"

Auden almost wanted to ask Shane what he'd meant by that, but he didn't. It was only their first date after all. He didn't want to ruin it by asking a stupid question. Instead, he glanced around.

They were at the summit of the mountain, and although they were alone, they had passed plenty of people on the way up. "We're a little out in the open, and if you think I'm iffy about sitting on a rock, I'm definitely not getting on the ground."

Shane paused for a second and laughed. "Not that kind of stress relief," he said. "Not yet."

Ducking his head, Auden felt the flush on his cheeks again. It wasn't like him to suggest something like that, but it had partially been a joke. It was so much easier with Trayce, he found himself thinking as Shane settled in across from him. He wouldn't have even had to make an awkward joke, but a part of him was glad Shane hadn't brought him up here just to fool around. Shane was different, very different from Trayce. He knew he shouldn't compare them— they were worlds apart—but he wondered if Trayce would ever do something like this. It was stupid. He shook himself. He was here with Shane, not Trayce, and he shouldn't be thinking about someone else.

"You ready?" Shane asked as Auden pulled himself together. He was on a date with Shane. That was who he should be thinking of.

"Yeah," he replied finally. He would be.

Heading back from the shower, Auden wasn't sure how he was supposed to feel. He'd left Shane at the trailhead that afternoon with the promise of a phone call and a short, too brief, kiss. It wasn't how Auden had imagined a first date ending, but he supposed that was how normal dates went. How would he know? He had nothing to compare it to.

"Hey."

Auden looked up as he passed Trayce. Trayce was wearing a pair of jeans and a tank top from his training, whereas Auden had thrown on a pair of soft fleece pants after his shower. It had been a cool shower after the warmth of the day, though it hadn't been cold enough to suppress the stirring he felt as he glanced at Trayce.

"You didn't come to training."

"It's optional," Auden pointed out, but he knew full well that anyone aiming for the Olympics didn't see it that way. He'd probably get an earful from Dorian on Monday.

Trayce smiled, shaking his head. "Tell Dorian that. Where were you?"

"I just went out." He wasn't sure why but it felt weird to tell

Trayce that he'd been out on a date. Trayce probably would have laughed at him. He paused, watching the way Trayce cocked a hip to the side, a curious tilt to his head, and Auden knew he was going to ask more questions. Auden nodded at his dorm room. Trayce followed him in without a word. They could at least do it where not everyone could hear.

Chapter 5
Date-able

Inside the dorm, Auden shut the door and flicked on the light. It was still light outside, but the sun was starting to sink outside the window. The air conditioner hummed under the ledge and Auden dropped down on his bed. Trayce joined him, scooting back easily.

"You know, it's kind of creepy to have a picture of your coach in your dorm," he said, nodding at the photo of the 2008 Olympic team.

"You have a picture of Jules in yours." Auden had seen it stuck up on the closet door that Trayce never bothered to close—a shirtless picture no less, of Jules in his glory days.

"He was hot. He is hot."

"Don't let Dorian hear you say that." Auden paused. They were close enough that he could reach out and touch Trayce's hand if he wanted to, but he'd probably only get a raised eyebrow if he tried. Friends. They were friends, not boyfriends. "When did you know?"

"That Jules was hot?" Trayce sat back, biting his lip as he thought. "Probably right around the 2016 Olympics. I was only twelve at the time but I knew if I ever had an older guy fetish, I'd pick Jules. Besides, he was in three consecutive Olympics—the guy's got talent."

"I meant, when did you know you wanted to be an Olympian."

"Forever," Trayce replied as though it should have been obvious. "I don't know. It wasn't like I woke up one morning and was like, I want to spend the next ten years of my life falling on my ass for a tiny scrap of metal. Why? You getting scared I'll beat you on the team?"

"You wish," Auden tried to joke but he couldn't deny the feeling of unease that followed. Maybe he did want Trayce to beat him. At least then he'd have a valid excuse for not making the team.

Trayce paused at his answer. "Are you okay? You've been acting weird."

"I'm fine," Auden assured him. "I'd be more fine if we could stop talking."

"Oh, I get it," Trayce said, shifting towards Auden, a smile creeping onto his face. "You're just using me for my body."

"Shut up." Auden rolled his eyes, but he watched Trayce scoot over, their arms brushing now, and it sent a thrill through him. It hadn't been like this with Shane. It was so much easier with Trayce who didn't even have to ask what he was thinking, who just knew what he wanted him to do.

"It's okay," Trayce replied, lifting a hand to Auden's face and turning it to face him. His thumb slid down his jaw, and if Auden closed his eyes, he could almost imagine it was more than just an empty gesture. "I don't mind."

Trayce kissed Auden, slow and steady, fingers sliding into his hair to drag him closer. His lips were soft and warm, an easy pressure against Auden's mouth as Trayce moved, pushing Auden onto his back. Closing his eyes, Auden kissed him back, opening his mouth to Trayce's and letting him deepen the kiss.

Most of the time, Trayce didn't bother with kissing too much. It took away from the rest of it, he said, got in the way of the fun part, but now, he took his time. Auden couldn't really think, not with Trayce's tongue sliding along his bottom lip, the warm ghost of breath over his skin that made his toes curl. All he could do was move his hand to Trayce's shoulder, bunching the thin fabric of his shirt, pulling him closer.

Not four hours ago, he'd been sitting on top of a mountain with Shane, and now he was underneath Trayce, blood rushing to his cock. The thought only gave him a moment's pause when Trayce slid down to mouth at his neck, his touch too light to leave marks since they both knew the consequences and neither wished to face Dorian's disapproving glare. Auden encouraged him with a moan, his hand sliding to Trayce's hair and tightening in the locks. All thoughts of Shane vanished with Trayce's tongue sliding over his throat.

Trayce's hands moved from Auden's hair, leaving it thoroughly mussed, and dropped to his waist, pushing under his old tee shirt instead. His fingers curled against Auden's stomach, thumbs pressing into his hips, and his breath was hot against Auden's neck.

Auden wasn't ready to lose Trayce's mouth quite yet, and he pulled Trayce back up for another kiss, sloppy and hard, something he desperately needed.

"Hey, relax," Trayce mumbled a second later, forcefully slowing him down with short kisses until they reached a leisurely pace.

It was easy for Trayce, easy to take his time and not think about whether this meant anything. It didn't to him, Auden knew. It was just getting off, but Auden could pretend.

Trayce's tongue curled against his, teeth grazing along his bottom lip, and Auden shifted. He was already hard—he'd been halfway there since he'd left Shane earlier—and he could feel the pressure of Trayce's body above him. Reaching down, Auden slid his hands over Trayce's ass, dragging his hips down to grind against his.

"Fuck, Auden," Trayce breathed, nipping at his jaw. "Your outing made you hot or what?" He said it with a laugh in his voice, but he shoved up Auden's shirt a second later, too quickly to be anything other than eager. It came over Auden's head with a slight struggle, ending up gracelessly on the floor. "We should do this more often."

Auden could only groan, hands pushing under Trayce's shirt, rucking it up to his shoulder blades. His hands slid over Trayce's shoulders, feeling the strain of his muscles. His knees came up to bracket Trayce on top of him, hips meeting in a rush of heat that made Trayce let out a soft noise, barely an exhale.

At least Auden knew he could get that kind of response from Trayce. He might never get lingering touches in public or kisses on the cheek after practice, but he could make Trayce moan and gasp above him and that was something.

Auden pulled at Trayce's shirt, getting it over his head. Reaching down, he nudged Trayce's hips away from his, tearing down Trayce's zipper and shoving his jeans over his hips. Trayce helped him out, pushing them off.

It took Trayce less time to yank Auden's pants down, no zipper to bother with. "God," he breathed, pushing Auden's knees apart and reaching for his cock. "Do you have—"

Auden bit his lip and stretched back, groping on the desk crammed next to the bed. He jerked the top drawer open, rummaging blindly for lube and box of condoms.

"Here," he panted, shaking one out.

Trayce grabbed the condom, ripping it open with his teeth and shedding the wrapper.

Auden exhaled, looking up at Trayce as Trayce reached down, rolling on the condom. He watched the way Trayce's eyes dropped, low and hooded, mouth falling open as he breathed. His eyes scraped over Trayce's chest, down to his hips and the trail of hair leading down to his prick.

There was no denying that Trayce was good-looking, but all gymnasts had great bodies, Auden thought, distracted by the sculpted muscles of Trayce's stomach as Trayce flipped open the lube and covered his fingers.

"Shit!" Auden gasped as Trayce slid his fingers in, two to start with, not giving him much time to prepare.

He panted for breath, shifting around Trayce's fingers, his legs pushed up near his head, and it was a good thing he was so flexible. Trayce's shoulder braced the back of his thigh, his fingers pushing in deeper, dragging against the muscles inside.

They'd gotten past the handjobs and blowjobs fairly early on, bypassing the awkwardness of sucking each other off. It had become so easy, so simple, everything Auden wished it would be, except with someone who would do more afterward than ask about his schedule for next week's training. For a second, when Trayce's eyes flicked to his, Auden's mind flashed to earlier with Shane, when Shane had smiled at him from across the rock.

Should this have been Shane? A part of Auden was glad it was Trayce, though. With Shane, it would have been awkward, different, new, all the things he didn't have to worry about with Trayce. He gasped a second later, eyes squeezing shut as Trayce dragged his fingers out and replaced them with his cock, hot and hard, pressing inside him. Trayce knew exactly what to do to bring him to the edge.

He could barely swallow, heat filling him, Shane's smile vanished from his mind as Trayce filled him. Instead, he could only feel Trayce, the way he pushed in and drew back, torturously slow, then slid back in. The whole bed shook, inching back against the carpeted floor.

Auden gasped, reaching for Trayce's sides, biting his lip, but he opened his mouth to Trayce's as Trayce smashed their mouths together, his hips rocking in hard.

The kiss was unfinessed, mostly panted breath and lips sliding together, and Auden's hand wrapped around the back of Trayce's neck to stop him from pulling away. Their bodies moved together, knocking the bed against the wall, an uneven rhythm. Auden swallowed hard, panting against Trayce's mouth, pushing his hips against Trayce's, copying his rhythm and groaning when Trayce's hand closed around his cock and pulled.

He wasn't going to make it much longer, not with Trayce's hand, still slick with lube, jerking him off. A dull flush crept up his collarbone, decorating his cheeks as he sucked in a breath. He could feel his legs shaking, the ache in his ass growing with each push of Trayce's hips. His cock throbbed in Trayce's grip.

He whined softly with the last push of Trayce's hips, feeling the way they stuttered, Trayce's sharp breath, the way he breathed out afterward, his hips slowing, pushing in and out more leisurely.

"Trayce," Auden tried to warn him, to keep his hand going as it slowed as well. He needed to get off, and Trayce wasn't always good at follow-through, not when it came to this.

Luckily, Trayce heeded his unspoken request, dragging his palm against Auden's cock, slower and then faster. His hips finally drew to a stop but his hand didn't, working Auden up to a point where he could hardly take a breath longer than a gasp, panting, his fingers digging into the back of Trayce's neck.

"Fuck," he gasped finally, eyes squeezing shut as his body reacted, his stomach tightening and the heat crashing over him as he came.

He felt Trayce sliding out as he came, the ache that remained. Trayce's hand stroked him through it, and he forced his eyes open, meeting Trayce's gaze as he panted for breath and finally sighed long and slow. Licking his lips, his hand slid from Trayce's neck, falling to the bed.

Trayce let his legs down finally, looking around for something to clean up with. He grabbed an old towel from the floor, wiping off his hand then handing it to Auden. Auden lay there for a moment, breathing slowly.

"Where'd you go?" Trayce asked after a minute. "A strip club?"

"In the middle of the day?" Auden replied skeptically, and Trayce shrugged, lying back down and setting his hands on his stomach.

"You don't usually skip out on practice."

"I..." He hesitated, debating whether or not he really wanted to tell Trayce. "I went on a date."

There was a pause then Trayce said, "Really?"

Auden frowned. "You don't believe me?"

"No, I'm sure you did. You're very date-able."

Date-able, but Trayce didn't want to date him.

"What's that supposed to mean?"

Trayce shrugged again and smiled slightly as Auden propped himself up on his elbow so he could look at him easier. "Nothing. You're a nice, cute, good-looking guy."

"That's it?" Auden asked, underwhelmed by his reaction.

"What do you want me to say, Auden? You want me to get jealous? To storm around like a kid whose candy got stolen? That's not gonna happen."

Yes, that was exactly what Auden wanted. He wanted some kind of proof that Trayce cared about him and his dating habits, even if it had only been one date and they'd spent most of it climbing a steep hill in the blazing sun.

"Why not?"

Trayce pushed himself up into a sitting position, facing Auden, and shook his head. "We've been over this. Relationships are just an excuse to use someone else to fix your problems, but they usually create more problems than they solve. Just look at all the divorced people in the world. Look at my parents. They were a real model for healthy relationships—screaming constantly—they were only really happy once they divorced."

"Not everyone is like your parents," Auden pointed out. "Plenty of people have good relationships."

"Maybe," Trayce admitted. "But there's also the added problem of distractions. What you and I have, it fits in perfectly to our lives. There's no drama, there's nothing that takes away from training. It's getting off and having a good time doing it. If we started dating, it would just be, ugh." He made a face. "Look, I want to go to the Olympics, and I know you do too, and now is not the time to start wanting relationships with anyone."

It was so matter-of-fact that Auden couldn't argue with him. Of course, he had a point. Now wasn't the time to start something like this, but it still hurt that Trayce hadn't even bothered to think about it. Trials were just another excuse not to do things, just like everything else.

Trayce sighed as they sat there a minute longer then leaned forward and pressed a kiss to Auden's lips. He pulled back and held his gaze for a moment. "Like I said, you're very date-able. I wouldn't worry."

As Trayce gathered his clothes and redressed, Auden was left with an ache in his chest that had nothing to do with training for once.

Auden sailed through the air off the vault, hands leaving and twisting tight to his body as he moved, but he felt it before it happened, the momentum running out mid-twist, and he landed on the mat, stumbling forward onto his knees. Pushing himself up, he silently cursed the vault behind him.

"You know what you did wrong?" Dorian asked as Auden grabbed a towel and wiped the sweat off his face.

"Opened up too late," he muttered.

"Opened up too late," Dorian repeated seriously. "Rookie mistake, Auden. This isn't even your most difficult vault. It's not about difficulty; it's about how well you pull it off. If you have an easier vault, it better be flawless."

Vault had never been Auden's strongest suit, and it was especially difficult when his coach had been one of the best vaulters in the entire world at one point.

"How about you show me?" he tried to joke, but Dorian pursed his lips.

"Funny. Back to the start and watch your core this time."

At the start of the mat, Auden paused to take a deep breath. It wasn't a long run to the vault, but it seemed to stretch before him as he stood there. It was just a vault. He'd done it a million times before. This was no different except that every attempt was one step closer to the Olympics. No pressure.

Wiping chalk on his hands, Auden shook himself. Just focus, he told himself firmly. Focus and don't think about everything else. The only important thing right now was to get it right.

He started down the mat, building speed until he hit the vault, pushing off and sailing through the air—three twists—and his feet hit the mat with a stumbling force, but he managed to stay upright this time. The first time he'd tried vault, he hadn't even gotten enough momentum to make a full turn, but that was years ago. He hadn't received a much better expression from his coach at the time.

Dorian had his arms crossed. "Better, but I need you to explode off that vault. Do you understand what I'm saying?"

Auden nodded, but his head felt heavy as he did so. He understood perfectly what Dorian was saying, but listening was one thing—executing it was entirely another.

"You're talented," Dorian said, "but talent isn't the only thing that's gonna get you to the Olympics. Now, I'd keep practicing. Loosen up a little."

Auden thought it was a little ironic, Dorian telling him to loosen up, but he didn't say so. After all, Dorian was his coach, not his friend, and he had to listen to his advice. Dorian knew what he was doing—he'd already made it to the Olympics, and Auden didn't doubt that if it hadn't been for his injury, he would have gone to many more.

"Besides," Dorian said, gazing across the room at where Trayce was being spotted on the rings. "You'll want to have it down when your parents come."

"Parents?" Auden looked up sharply.

Dorian frowned at his question. "Your dad said they were coming down to see your practice. I assumed you were aware."

Auden didn't know what to say or why his chest tightened at the idea of seeing his parents right now. He tried to think of something quickly that would reassure Dorian. "Oh, yeah, I just forgot. Been busy with training and everything."

Something about Dorian's expression told Auden he didn't quite believe him, but thankfully, he didn't push.

"It's fine, them coming to visit," he said at length, "but I don't want you getting distracted this late in the game."

"Right." Auden nodded, quirking a brief smile. Of all the distractions Auden could have imagined, his parents hadn't been one. It wasn't as though there was necessarily anything wrong with them visiting, but it was so much easier when they were in San Diego, where they didn't have to watch his progress and comment on everything that happened. Auden knew exactly what would happen once they got to Phoenix. His mom would be so impressed with everything and his father would comment on how expensive the equipment seemed.

Dorian was gazing at Trayce again, and Auden followed his eyes. Trayce was a much better distraction, one he'd much prefer to think about rather than the impending trials and the pressure that made him constantly feel as though one good stumble on a mat would end his chances for good—and he wasn't sure if that made him happy or not.

Dorian snapped back to him a second later, though. "Let's run it again, and I don't want to see any missteps."

Auden nodded, but he deflated slightly when Dorian turned away. At this point, Auden wasn't sure he had anything but missteps left.

Chapter 6
The Countdown Begins

"Pick up, pick up, pick up," Auden muttered into the phone as he left the gym and crossed the wide open space between it and the dorms. Other training buildings spotted the area — an Olympic-size swimming pool and diving pool — and beige pathways wound through the painstakingly-landscaped desert between them. The phone rang and rang again as Auden walked.

"Auden!" His mother answered at long last, sounding cheerful as she always did when he called. He supposed that meant he should call more often. "What a nice surprise."

"So, I hear you're coming down," he said, skipping straight to the point. He had no patience for pleasantries at this stage, and she'd just dance around him if he didn't ask directly anyway.

"Yes," his mom agreed. "Your father and I thought we'd come visit this weekend. We'll be up on Friday. That's not an inconvenience, is it?"

Auden grimaced but he couldn't say that it was. They were his parents, after all. They were the ones who paid for all this training. They expected he would make something of it — it just made him feel guilty whenever he contemplated the upcoming trials and whether or not this was really what he wanted.

"No, of course not," he said through gritted teeth. "I just wish you'd told me."

"We wanted it to be a surprise," she said, but there was a muffled scuffle a second later and the voice of his sister came through the receiver instead.

"Auden, guess what!"

"Hey, Clover."

"I'm starting level four next week! Someday I'm gonna go to the Olympics just like you!"

Auden forced himself to laugh. "Yeah? Think you've got a few years to go." More like eight years until she'd even be old enough to qualify. Still, he wondered if she'd still be so interested once she realized that it meant sacrificing a normal childhood for one moment. Some days, Auden wasn't sure it had been worth it.

He could hear her sticking out her tongue at him through the receiver from the sound she made. "When you go to France, Daddy says we're gonna record it so we can save it for always! Why can't we go see you in the Olympics?"

"I'm not in the Olympics yet," Auden said, though he knew it was futile. She was only eight years old—and she couldn't be talked out of whatever idea she had in her head. If she thought he was going to the Olympics, he was going to the Olympics. "And it's expensive to fly across the world."

"But you're going!"

Auden didn't know what to say, and he was glad when his mother wrestled the phone away from Clover.

"Honey, give that back," he heard her say and then she was back. "Auden, we'll be down on Friday. I know your dad would like to see the facilities again, so maybe you could put together a little tour?"

Auden knew what that meant, and he mentally made a note to look up the expense report for the Center. Already, he dreaded being grilled on the cost of equipment and the coaches' salaries. Why couldn't his dad just be normal?

"Sure," he muttered. Clearly, this was happening and there was no stopping it. At least he had a few days to prepare, but considering every minute counted, a few days was little more than a blip.

"Okay, we'll see you soon!" his mother said over Clover's whining to give back the phone. She hung up before Clover could steal it back, and Auden sighed, sliding his phone into his bag.

He reached the dorms and stepped into the shadow of the front overhang, out of the blistering sun, pausing against a pillar. The thought of seeing his parents wasn't reassuring. If anything, it made him feel worse. They'd be expecting him to be excited, to have everything planned out for trials, and at the moment, he wasn't sure how he felt about any of it.

"Who kicked you today?" Trayce stepped under the overhang, his bag over his shoulder, sweatpants slung low on his hips.

Auden really wasn't in the mood to explain how everything in his life seemed to be spiraling downward, but he met Trayce's gaze. "My parents are coming to visit."

"That's... not good?" Trayce asked uncertainly. "Thought you liked your parents."

"I do. It's just." He paused, glancing at Trayce. He could tell him the real reason: that the thought of his parents coming and seeing everything and being so sure that he was going to make the team, being so confident in everything, more confident than him, that it made him feel sick. It made him feel physically sick when he thought of all the people who were so sure he was going to make it. How could they know something like that? How could they be so blindly believing? He could tell Trayce that, but he didn't. Instead, he shrugged. "I just need to focus on training right now."

Trayce bobbed his head. "Well, at least your parents can stand to be in the same room together. If I make the team, mine'll have to sit at opposite ends of the gym."

"I guess there's that," Auden muttered, but it didn't make him feel much better.

Trayce smiled slightly. "Some of the guys were thinking of going to see a movie tonight, but if you were tired from training, we could probably make some kind of excuse." Stepping forward, he reached out for Auden's waist, his touch falling down his side, light but purposeful.

Auden paused at Trayce's offer. He didn't even bother to veil his intentions anymore, not like when they'd first gotten together. It was an offer Auden would usually take in a second—anything to get Trayce away from his usual bravado and naked. The offer meant nothing to Trayce, though, just an excuse to get off instead of seeing some over-priced movie in a freezing cold theater.

"I think I'm just gonna rewatch some old Olympic recordings tonight. Enjoy the movie," Auden said, pushing off the pillar and heading for the door.

"Auden?" Trayce said from behind him, frowning at him, but Auden didn't glance back despite the confused tone of his voice, something he rarely heard.

What Auden really needed right now was someone who knew nothing about gymnastics.

"I was surprised you called me," Shane said, rounding the couch and handing Auden a glass of water. He took his seat next to him and pulled his guitar into his lap.

Auden was a little surprised as well, and he hadn't expected his call to Shane to end up with him in Shane's apartment at nine o'clock at night. Shane had invited him to come 'hang out,' though, so that was what he was doing.

"Didn't think I would?" It was weird, being in someone's apartment that he barely knew. He did barely know Shane. They'd been out once, and Auden wasn't sure it had gone well enough to call it a success.

The apartment was a small, beige sort of place, the walls hung with black and white pictures of concerts and an amp set up in the corner, cords tumbling over themselves. Out on the small balcony, a wilting plant sat shriveled in its pot.

"Honestly? No," Shane admitted. "You didn't really seem that into it."

Auden had no one to blame but himself for that, although he did put some of it on Trayce, or at least the thoughts of Trayce that always crept in whenever he was with Shane.

He glanced down at the glass of water in his hands. "I haven't been on a lot of dates," he said finally. "I haven't done much other than train for the past ten years of my life, so when a cute guy asks me out, I don't really know what to do."

"There's a lot more to life than training." Shane strummed a chord on his guitar.

"Not if you ask anyone at the Center."

"Well, we're not at the Center," Shane pointed out, smiling easily at Auden. He had a five o'clock shadow. "No coaches or team-mates here. So why don't you tell me why you waited so long to call?"

Auden hesitated a moment, staring at Shane. Shane wasn't going to let him off easy for this one, so he might as well just say it.

"It has almost nothing to do with you," he said at length. "I've been training to be a gymnast for over ten years, and this year, it's finally my shot to make it all worthwhile, but instead of being excited, I feel like it's strangling me. Everyone is so convinced I'm going to make it, and I just know it'll break their hearts if I don't."

"What if you got injured?"

Auden frowned. Normally, he tried not to think about injuries. Thinking about it usually cursed people. "Then I'd be injured." He didn't get what Shane meant.

"So break your leg," Shane suggested, plucking out a chord on his guitar. "Sprain an ankle. Then you're home free. It's an easy out."

"I don't want to get injured," Auden said slowly. That wouldn't solve his problem. It would just put him in pain and he'd still have to listen to everyone lamenting—probably for the rest of his life—what he could have done. That was almost worse.

Shane set his guitar aside and turned more towards Auden on the couch. "Alright, I'll take that answer."

"What?"

Shane's hand moved to Auden's knee, warm and heavy through the fabric of his jeans. Auden swallowed slowly, eyes flicking from his hand to Shane's face.

"Let's stop talking about gymnastics. I thought you were going to tell me there was someone else." Shane laughed. "Sports can be quit but getting someone else out of your head isn't as easy."

Auden's mind immediately flew to Trayce, Trayce's offer earlier, the one he'd turned down. He wasn't even sure why he had, even with Shane's hand pressing on his knee.

He hesitated. He wanted to be honest with Shane, but the thought of admitting what Trayce was to him—whether confusing or not—made him pause.

"Well," he said finally, nerves jangling up into his fingers. "There is someone... I mean, just someone I've kind of been..." He trailed away, staring at Shane's hand on his knee, scared of what he might see if he lifted his gaze.

"It's okay," Shane said, to Auden's surprise. He glanced up to find Shane watching him steadily. "We barely know each other."

"Oh." Auden felt a wave of relief that Shane wasn't upset, but right along with it came disappointment that Shane didn't care, just like Trayce hadn't.

"But I tend to be a one person kind of guy, so if, after a few more dates, you want to get serious, you'll have to be too."

Auden's disappointment vanished, replaced with giddy excitement, but it was tempered by the thought of stopping things with Trayce. Whatever he said, the sex was good and he definitely liked Trace in a way that was more than friends. He found himself nodding, though, at Shane.

Shane smiled easily, and something in Auden's chest tightened. He barely had enough time to prepare himself before Shane leaned over and kissed him.

It was different than Trayce's kisses, softer and slower, the rough scrape of stubble against Auden's chin. For a second, he wasn't sure what to do, but he kissed back slowly, closing his eyes to the drag of Shane's lips against his.

"Good," Shane murmured as he lowered Auden onto his back and kissed him again. Auden wasn't sure 'good' was the word he would use to describe the situation, but the most he wanted to do right now was kiss Shane and forget about everything else.

Auden felt better after his time with Shane, and he found himself back in the dorm hallways well after curfew. They'd only ended up watching a movie on the couch, Shane's arm around his shoulders, for the rest of the night. As much as it could have been awkward, it hadn't been as bad as he'd guessed.

Down the hallway, Auden passed Trayce's room. He paused as he stood there. It would have been so easy to keep walking, but it would have been more difficult to swallow the feeling of disappointment rising in him. Somehow, he'd made a promise to Shane, one he'd never made to anyone else. Even if they weren't serious right now, they might be soon and he'd have to stop things with Trayce.

Trayce wouldn't care, he told himself sharply, turning to continue to his room, but he couldn't make himself go on.

Stepping forward, he knocked on the door but there was no response. "Trayce?" he asked quietly, leaning in to listen.

The hallway was silent around him, too late for people to be up. On the off-chance he was lucky, Auden reached for the doorknob. It twisted open, unlocked. He'd never done this before, and Trayce would probably accuse him of losing it, but he stepped in anyway. He wanted to talk to Trayce, to somehow prove to himself that Trayce wasn't the emotionally-stunted guy he'd known for the past three years.

Inside the room, it was dark, the curtain dragged shut against the sun that would blaze in too early in the morning. Auden hesitated a moment before stepping inside and shutting the door. He could barely make out anything in the dark, but he moved towards where the bed should have been. It was stupid, he knew, coming here after being with Shane. Trayce was probably asleep and here he was creeping around his room.

"Trayce?" he asked again, quietly, as he reached the bed. His eyes adjusted slowly, making out the dark lump that was Trayce. It rustled, covers shifting.

"Auden?" Trayce asked, voice rough with sleep, confused and slurred. "What the hell are you doing?"

"I just wanted to talk to you—" Auden started to say, but Trayce groaned softly.

"What?"

Auden hesitated. This had been a stupid idea. There was nothing that Trayce would say that could assuage his guilt over choosing Shane. He had chosen Shane, hadn't he? If Trayce could be something else, someone else, someone who cared, maybe they could be more. He was just making excuses, though. The reason he liked Trayce wasn't because he was overly romantic. Trayce was practical and logical and he had a point about the whole distractions thing.

"I was just thinking about the date I went on. What if I like this guy?"

Trayce was silent for a minute, squinting up at Auden through the darkness. "Auden, shut up," he mumbled finally, scooting over on the bed and gesturing vaguely at him. "Get in."

It hadn't been what Auden had been expecting, but what had he been expecting? He honestly didn't know anymore. Toeing off his shoes, he slid onto the small bed next to Trayce, like a child afraid of the monsters in his room. Trayce rolled over, a hand sliding over Auden's waist. Butterflies erupted deep inside his chest, but Auden said nothing. Trayce was half-asleep, he told himself firmly.

"You already have people who like you," Trayce murmured against his neck, half an exhale.

Closing his eyes, Auden breathed in deeply. Tomorrow he'd have to figure this out, but for now, he'd rather lie there in Trayce's arms.

"T-minus forty-nine days," Anya said as she watched Auden do his stretches.

Auden rolled his eyes at the mat as he grabbed his ankles and held the pose for fifteen seconds. He really didn't need a countdown, not when there was one constantly ticking in the back of his mind.

"Shouldn't you be watching your own team practice?" he asked instead, stretching his shoulders.

Anya shrugged. "It's far less depressing to watch you boys. At least I can root for you to make the team. Watching my friends practice is like putting a nail in my own coffin. Plus, there's the added bonus of toned asses and well-muscled chests if I stay here."

She was talking about Liam, Auden knew, glancing over to where Liam was doing his stretches, his shirt long gone. Shaking his head, he returned to his own warm-up.

"And people think gymnasts are shallow."

"Everyone is to some degree," she replied, propping her elbows on her knees and dropping her chin in her hands. "You wouldn't fool around with Trayce otherwise."

"That's not true," Auden argued, though he purposefully didn't look around for Trayce. After the other night, neither had said anything about it. Trayce had already been gone when Auden woke up, and he had seemed to elect to pretend it hadn't happened. Auden had spent the next couple of days going over Trayce's words, re-playing them, but he couldn't tell if they meant that Trayce liked him, or if it had just been sleep mumbling.

Anya arched an eyebrow at his response. "Right, you admire his prowess at that stupid video game so much you just had to sleep with him."

"We're friends," Auden insisted.

"You play video games, you watch movies. You share an obses-sion with the same sport. That makes you friends. What makes you more than friends is the part where you take each other's clothes off and spend too much time staring at his ass."

Auden felt his cheeks going red but he glared at Anya. "I do not."

"You do," she replied simply. "And it's perfectly fine as long as you admit that your interest in him doesn't just verge on the phys-ical."

"I just said it didn't. You're the one who argued."

Anya leaned forward. "And that's the problem."

"What's the problem?"

Auden didn't see what she was getting at, and he had enough to worry about with his parents showing up in a few hours. For the next forty-eight hours, he had to pretend that everything was great, and it was going to take all of his strength to do it.

"You like him but he doesn't like you back."

"He likes me," Auden said, frowning.

"Not like you do. He likes sleeping with you. He likes playing video games with you, but he doesn't want to date you or hold your hand or any of that stuff."

"What's it to you?" Auden snapped. He was getting pretty tired of other people defining his and Trayce's relationship. He couldn't even figure it out most of the time, so how could they even begin to? "You're not sleeping with him."

Anya sat up at his tone and brushed her hair back. "You're for-ty-nine days away from something monumental and I don't want you to screw it up."

"Thanks for the vote of confidence." He said it, but despite the sarcasm, he just felt angry. His whole life hinged on one moment and that would make or break him. Where he had once been excited, he now hated the feeling. How could he be sure this was what he even wanted? Maybe everyone else just wanted it for him.

"You know what I mean," she said with a sigh. "You're gonna be an Olympian as long as you stay focused for forty-nine days."

Forty-nine days wasn't that long, but to Auden, it could have been an eternity.

Chapter 7
Parental Influence

Auden wasn't sure how much longer he could listen to his dad debate the prices of all the equipment in the gym. It had already been an hour of, "I bet that costs more than my annual salary" and "You know, Auden, it would almost be cheaper to send you to a private university than to train here."

Swallowing down the annoyance, Auden pushed open the doors of the gym to the courtyard, his parents following. As much as he generally liked his parents, he wasn't a kid anymore and putting up with them was less a requirement and more a grudging respect. After all, they did pay for his training, but he didn't feel as though he needed to be reminded of that fact every time he talked to them.

"It's so much prettier than I remember," his mother said as they crossed the landscaped desert. The last time they had come had been the end of summer two years ago, when the temperatures had been in the low hundreds and everything had been dried up and dead. Now, remnants of spring still lingered in the flowering cacti, the millions of yellow flowers on the Mesquite trees. There were even hints of green among the sandy brown. The warm breeze fluttered his mother's stringy brown hair, the same shade as both Auden's and his dad's, although his dad's was streaked with grey. He said it came from the financial stress of paying for the Center.

"Hmph," his dad muttered, glancing around. "They spend a lot on irrigation, don't they?" He straightened his suit jacket, the button closed neatly over his wiry frame.

"I have no idea," Auden replied, trying not to roll his eyes. He should have been happy that they were here to see him, but instead, he just wanted it to be over. He wanted to escape to his dorm and watch a movie he'd seen a thousand times. It would be better than reliving the cost of everything out here.

"I looked into San Diego State, you know," his dad went on as though Auden hadn't spoken. "It really would be cheaper to send you there."

"Are you saying that because you want me to go to college or because you don't think I'll make the team?"

It was a loaded question, he knew, but he wanted to know their answer. Maybe if they didn't think he would make it, he could just quit. For a second, he almost felt hopeful, but his mother shook her head, hair falling out of her bun.

"That's ridiculous," she assured him with a hand on his arm. "We've known since the very first time you climbed up on that jungle gym and did a backflip off it that you would be a great gymnast. It's just... the cost can be restrictive." She shot a look at his dad. "But we know you're going to make it all worth it. If it makes you happy, it's worth it. We've already started looking up flights to Paris for this summer. Do you know if family get special seats or do we have to buy tickets like everyone else?"

Auden's heart sank. It could have been much worse, he tried to remind himself. He could want this so badly and they could be unsupportive.

"I don't know," he said. "It's a little early to be planning, though."

"Trials are just around the corner!" she said eagerly, linking her arm with his as they watched. "Soon enough the world will know what we have all along—that you are a great athlete."

His father made another noise, kicking a rock off the pathway in front of him. "Your mother's right. It'll be worth it in the end. Although, with all that new equipment in that gym, I hope they're spending my hard-earned dollars well."

Auden didn't mention that his dad wasn't exactly poor. He had a fairly successful career as a data analyst back in San Diego. He just had a tight hold on the purse strings. There were other people who had it far worse, like Trayce who had to convince his parents to work together to pay for things. It wasn't as easy for him.

They neared the dorms, the sun beating down on them, hot and dry. Maybe he could leave them and have some time to himself.

"We know you're going to be great," his mother said easily. "We have no doubts that you're going to make the team."

It didn't make Auden feel better. If anything, it made him feel worse. He couldn't explain why, but he hated that they had so much confidence. They were his parents, though; they had to be like that.

"Auden, hey!" someone called from behind them as they approached the dorm overhang. Turning, he found Trayce coming towards him. He wasn't sure if he was glad for the distraction or nervous of what Trayce might say.

"Trayce," he said slowly as he reached them. Trayce quirked an eyebrow and smiled at his parents. It was easy and charming, something that came so naturally to him.

"You must be Mr. and Mrs. Lancaster," Trayce said, grin widening. "I'm Trayce."

"The Canadian," his dad said immediately. Auden frowned and looked away from him, meeting Trayce's curious gaze. "I'm surprised the Center allows foreigners to train here."

Trayce merely blinked in return. "Apparently my money is as good as yours."

Auden cursed to himself. This was not how he wanted his parent's first meeting with Trayce to go. If anything, he might have hoped for a pleasant exchange in which they came off with a favorable opinion of him. That didn't seem to be the case, though, and he wished his dad could just be quiet.

"And I'll be competing for a spot on the US team," Trayce went on.

His dad frowned but Auden's mother stepped in.

"That's wonderful," she said, squeezing his dad's arm purposefully. "Are you excited about your chances?"

Trayce crossed his arms over his chest, glancing at Auden, who wished he could just melt into the ground right about now. He was so sick of hearing about the Olympics. Every mention of it made his chest ache uncomfortably. Why couldn't they just stop talking about it?

"I'm not worried," Trayce said simply. "Besides, I've got Auden to keep me on track."

That made Auden's mom smile proudly, eyes gleaming with

that might have been tears, but Auden was immensely glad when she didn't cry.

"I'd say of everyone, Auden and I have the best shot of making the team. We've put in a lot of time, and Coach keeps our noses to the grindstone."

Beside Auden, his father shifted. "At least there's that," he muttered.

Auden tried to ignore him but it was difficult.

Trayce glanced at his dad. "Yeah, Auden and I have become pretty good friends." Auden wasn't sure if his parents caught it, but he certainly heard the slight emphasis on 'friends.' Judging from the way his father's jaw tightened, he had.

"We have to get going," Auden interrupted sharply, if only to stop his father from punching his teammate. That wouldn't look too good. Plus, as annoying as Trayce could be, he didn't deserve a fist in his face.

"It was lovely to meet you," his mother said as Auden practically dragged them off, away from the dorms. He didn't know where they were going, but somewhere far away from Trayce and his big mouth.

His father said nothing as they walked down the path, heading for the parking lot instead where the rental car was parked. Auden could feel the tension, the awkwardness lingering from Trayce's introduction.

"Who's hungry?" his mom piped in finally as they walked. "I'm ready for dinner, what do you boys say?"

Auden didn't reply, but his dad drew himself together a second later and nodded.

"Yes, let's find somewhere to eat."

Auden didn't suggest the cafeteria, and led the way to the parking lot instead.

The Rio Grille was about as tropical as north Scottsdale got, with a giant tiki in the front entrance, but the fried calamari was so good that Auden didn't even grimace at what Dorian might have said if he ever found out he snuck one off the appetizer plate. Little lights hung low over the tables, dim enough to feel like it was constantly nighttime inside the restaurant.

Something felt strange, though Auden couldn't put his finger on it. His dad had been unusually quiet since they'd left the Center. His mother had filled most of the conversation with comments on the desert plants and how she wanted to plant a Joshua Tree in their backyard at home.

Glancing between them across the table, Auden frowned. His dad poked at the fried squid on his plate with his fork, the edges of his mouth twitching occasionally like they did when he was working on a particularly difficult math problem. Auden's mother smiled as he looked to her for an answer.

"Clover wanted to come, but she's staying with your Aunt Rebecca instead," she said. "We thought it'd be nicer for just the two of us to come visit."

"Oh, right," Auden agreed. He barely knew his aunt, considering it had been years since he'd seen her. He didn't go home much now that he was at the Center except for holidays, and even then, he spent most of his time at the gym or on the beach when he was there.

"You know, we hardly get to see you these days," she went on. "Maybe you could train closer to home."

Auden hesitated, glancing at his dad again, but he remained silent, contemplating his plate deeply. "Well, EGC is the best Center on the west coast. Well, sort of west coast."

"Most expensive too," his dad muttered under his breath, but Auden tried to ignore him. He couldn't, though, when his dad sat up straighter and said, "That, uh, *friend*, of yours, the Canadian, how well do you know him?"

"Trayce, you mean?" Auden asked though he knew perfectly well his dad didn't care about his name.

His father grunted vaguely. "He didn't seem like the best influence."

Auden frowned. "What does that mean?"

"Your father just means that he, he's different," his mom piped in unhelpfully. She shot his dad a look that he grimaced at but seemingly ignored its meaning.

"Different," Auden repeated dimly. "Bad different?" He looked between his mother, who seemed apologetic, and his father, who chewed the inside of his cheek as though debating whether or not to say something. He seemed to decide to say it, though, setting down his fork with a clink.

"Auden, are you involved with that boy?"

"Oh my God," Auden muttered, covering his face, elbows on the table. This couldn't be happening. There were certain things he didn't discuss with his parents, and his love life, or lack thereof, was one of them.

"It's just a question," his father said gruffly, ruffling himself and staring imperiously across the table at Auden. "I don't think it's a good idea."

Auden lowered his hands. "Why? Because he's a guy or because he's Canadian?" If there was one part of his life he didn't need parental advice in, it was about guys.

"Don't be glib," his dad replied sharply. "Being involved with anyone isn't what I pay for you to come here for. You're here to train and that's all."

Auden pinched the bridge of his nose. He couldn't believe they were having this conversation. His mother was absolutely no help, drowning herself in her water glass instead. "I am training. All I do is train," he argued. "I don't have any friends outside the Center, Dad. How could I when this is my whole life?"

His answer didn't seem to appease his dad, but it was true. He didn't have time or the ability to make friends outside of the bubble he lived in. Shane was the only person he knew who wasn't obsessed with gymnastics, the only person who was somewhat normal, who had a life and goals and dreams outside of sports.

His dad frowned at Auden. "You're not here to make friends."

"So I can't be friends with the people on my team?"

"Friends, yes," he said firmly. "Not more than that. This boy—"

"Trayce."

"—he's not even American. How can he compete on the team? He'll be your competition."

"I know, Dad," Auden replied impatiently. "It doesn't matter that he's Canadian. If he's good, he deserves to be on the team." He didn't want to argue about Trayce. Trayce was confusing enough as it was. "Mom?"

She smiled easily. "This is a wonderful restaurant."

"Mom!" Auden needed more help than that. At least she didn't freak out at the idea of him being involved with someone.

"Honey, your father's just saying that you need to focus on yourself right now, not on anyone else." She straightened her silverware and avoided his frown.

"He just doesn't like Trayce because he's a guy."

"He was rude and disrespectful," his dad interrupted, but Auden shook his head.

"You were first. Trayce is one of the only people at the Center I actually get along with really well. He's not just another teammate. He's a great gymnast and he's got a really good shot of making the team." He said it as though Trayce making the team might make himself feel better about not wanting to make it.

"This isn't about you being gay," his dad said finally, lowering his voice as though someone might overhear. "It's just... inappropriate."

Auden frowned. Of course his dad thought it was inappropriate. His dad thought it was inappropriate to wear anything other than suits. A gay son wasn't his idea of perfect, especially a gay gymnast son.

His mother said nothing, though she did lay a hand on his dad's arm as though to calm him. Auden didn't understand why she didn't say anything, but her look seemed enough to stop his dad from saying anything else for the moment, though he frowned as though annoyed at her action. Wordless communication. At least they had that going for them. After all, they had been married for almost twenty-five years.

"We should order," she said, looking around for the server.

Reaching for his glass, Auden downed his water. Arguing about Trayce was not how he wanted to spend the evening, especially when his dad kept chewing on his cheek, as though mulling over all the things he could say.

Luckily for Auden, he stayed silent for the moment as the server came to take their order and refill their drinks.

"Why the hell did you have to do that?" Auden asked, pushing past Trayce into his room without waiting to be invited.

Trayce let him, an eyebrow raised. "Escaped your parents, I see."

"Trayce," Auden snapped, turning around. Trayce shut the door behind him and stepped over a pile of clothes on the floor.

"What?"

"You didn't have to be rude."

Trayce laughed sharply. "Because your dad was so polite to me, the foreigner. Are you sure you want to be in here? You might get the sudden urge to sing 'Oh Canada' and drink ale."

Rolling his eyes, Auden sighed. The rest of dinner had been filled with veiled references to why distractions were a bad thing, especially when his dad was paying for the best coaching in the country, not for him to fuck around with a Canadian.

"He's just concerned with anyone who could be competition." He didn't know why he was defending his dad.

"Yeah, right," Trayce scoffed. "He doesn't think anyone should be better than you, especially me. Maybe he'd like your boyfriend better."

That caught Auden off-guard. They still hadn't discussed the other night, and Trayce bringing it up unexpectedly threw him off. So Trayce had noticed, had remembered. He decided not to comment on it. It would probably just makes things worse.

"He just expects me to be the best." Auden felt bad enough, with his parents unwavering belief in his abilities. "You know, for a Canadian, you're not very nice." He frowned. "The day was going badly enough already and then you showed up and now he thinks you're a distraction from the competition."

Trayce almost laughed, kicking aside the pile of clothes and coming closer.

"Sorry to disappoint your stereotypes of how I should be. Am I really that big of a distraction for you, Auden? Can't keep it in your pants for ten minutes, huh?"

"That's not what I said." Auden didn't back down as Trayce approached, crossing his arms defensively. "It's bad enough that my dad likes to constantly remind me how much I cost him, but then he thinks I'm not focused and I have to listen to lectures on responsibility and priorities." Auden didn't know what his priorities were anymore, and getting lectured on them was not his idea of a good time.

"I've got your priorities right here," Trayce replied, pushing Auden back against the wall and trapping him there with the hard press of his body.

Auden wanted to be annoyed, but after days of awkwardness after that night, he was all too willing to pull Trayce in closer. His mind flitted vaguely to Shane, but they weren't serious. They hadn't talked about being serious. It had only been two semi-dates, and Trayce was the one staring at his mouth like he wanted to ravish him. It sent heat straight to his cock, and Auden couldn't have pushed Trayce away even if he'd wanted to.

"You can tell your dad that the Canadian is the one who gets you on your knees," Trayce murmured in his ear, a hand sneaking down his torso, fingernails scratching over his tee-shirt until he reached his jeans and cupped Auden's erection through the material. Auden took a quick breath but he didn't dare look down, not with Trayce's mouth hovering closer to his ear, breath feathering over his skin, warm and soft. "You can tell him that it's so easy, the way you take me. You're always so eager."

Auden shut his eyes and groaned as Trayce ground his hand against his cock. Already half-hard, he sighed at the hard friction. His hands on Trayce's waist tightened.

Leaning in, Trayce's mouth ghosted over his neck, nose brushing against his jaw, fingers not tight enough on his prick. "How much do you think he'd hate me if he knew I can make you come with only my mouth?"

Auden swallowed hard against the rush of heat spreading over his body. "Probably a lot, but I don't care what he thinks." It was so easy to get lost in this, in Trayce's touch, the brush of lips against his jaw. Before Trayce could say something else, Auden reached up and pulled him into a searing kiss.

It was a mess after that, no more whispers in his ear, no more teasing from Trayce as he pulled open Auden's jeans and shoved them down. Trayce's mouth was hot and reckless against Auden's, hard and wanting. It was everything Auden wanted. His chest tightened and his hands threaded through Trayce's hair, keeping him there, preventing him from moving until Trayce bit at his mouth.

Trayce's hand wrapped around his cock, warm and tight, a pressure that made him moan.

"I don't care what he thinks either," Trayce murmured, eyes flicking to Auden's for a second, and Auden felt his heart swell for a second, just for a moment at what Trayce might have meant. Trayce licked his lips a second later, though, and dropped his gaze. "So you want me to prove it?"

"Fuck yes," Auden breathed when Trayce slid his hand out of his pants and dropped to his knees. There was nothing else to say as Trayce landed on the floor, peeling his jeans all the way off. There weren't many times Trayce did this, but every time was like a particularly good Christmas present.

Auden's whole body was flushed, tingling where Trayce's mouth slid over his hip and down to his thigh, pushing his legs apart. He spent a few minutes leaving a mark against his skin, too close to his cock but not close enough for any kind of release in the tension now curled deep inside his stomach.

"Trayce, come on," he murmured finally, reaching for Trayce's head, trying to give him a hint that ended up more like just stroking his hair as Trayce slid his tongue over his skin, tracing the red mark on his inner thigh.

Trayce glanced up, eyes meeting Auden's, and he smirked, licking his lips. "Look, Ma, no hands," he promised, holding them up and leaning in to nuzzle Auden's cock.

Auden felt the spark all through his body at Trayce's breath against his skin, hot and throbbing. He was about to chastise Trayce for teasing, but then Trayce's mouth was there, warm and wet, sliding over his cock and sucking in a way that made Auden's hips buck up. Trayce's hands shoved them back, pinning him to the wall. Auden wasn't sure that counted as no hands, but he tried to keep still as Trayce sucked him off, raw and ready.

As he stood there, Auden's mind went blank. He didn't think of his parents or Shane. He only thought of Trayce's mouth, the feeling of bliss that encompassed him as the tension crackled deep inside him, so close to coming already. He barely kept it together when Trayce slid off to suck at his balls, sliding his tongue over the sensitive skin until all Auden wanted to do was whine and come all over his face.

"Almost there," Trayce murmured as he slid back in, lips stretching over Auden's cock. Auden could barely look down, knowing the sight of Trayce with his mouth stretched over his hard cock would be too much to handle. Instead, he pushed his hips up gently, and Trayce let him this time, making a noise in the back of his throat that made Auden's toes curl.

"Trayce, I-I'm gonna," was all he got out before he came, cock still in Trayce's mouth.

Trayce let him, let him push in with his hips, the slick slide too much to handle and Auden shuddered as he came. Closing his eyes, he leaned back against the wall to support himself as he heard Trayce spit into the trash can. When he opened his eyes, breathing heavily still, he saw Trayce wipe his mouth and sit back on his heels, looking winded himself.

Climbing to his feet, Trayce cocked his head to the side. "You want to tell your dad about that?"

"I'd rather not." Auden would rather never tell anyone about the way something stupid fluttered through him at Trayce's smile.

Trayce ruffled his hair, his smile soft as he gazed at Auden. For a moment, it felt like it was just the two of them, that Trayce might take his hand and they'd lay down and talk about nothing and everything for hours. For a moment, Shane didn't exist on the outer reaches of Auden's mind, and he thought, maybe, Trayce felt it too from the way he gazed at him.

But then Trayce stepped away, adjusting his jeans, and Auden didn't make any offers. Instead, he watched him cross to his bed and flop down. Pulling up his jeans, Auden buttoned them slowly. So much for his fantasies. Even in those moments where Trayce smiled at him like that, Auden knew he was just fooling himself into thinking there was something more.

"Oh," Trayce said as Auden opened the door. "When we both make the team, I want to be there when you tell your parents."

Auden shut the door behind him.

Chapter 8
Taking Charge

"I'm not sure this was the best idea," Auden said, glancing below him nervously. He didn't like the precarious position he found himself in, hanging half off the fake rock wall. From below him, Shane arched an eyebrow and laughed.

"Soon you'll be ready for the real thing."

The thought didn't reassure Auden but he hauled himself up to the next footing. When Shane had suggested rock climbing, he had said yes mostly because he wanted to get out of the gym and away from everyone who had anything to do with training. He wasn't sure, however, that rock climbing had been the best idea.

"You mean with scorpions and tarantulas lurking in every crevice? On a really high mountain?"

"You fling yourself off a balance beam every day and you're scared of heights?" Shane asked skeptically, but Auden shook his head.

"Only women do the beam."

"Whatever." Shane stared up at him. "You can't tell me you're scared of heights?"

"It's not the height; it's the falling off the height that worries me."

Auden was used to being high. He was used to flying through the air all the time, but it was different. There were mats to break his fall, spotters to slow down the impact if something went wrong. He spent years practicing skills so he wouldn't fall flat on his face. It wasn't at all the same to climb up a vertical wall with little more than a rope to catch him if he fell. He definitely didn't trust the thin elastic rope supposedly keeping him safe.

Shane pulled the rope through the belay as Auden remained paused on the wall. He didn't want to go any higher, not until he could convince himself that he wasn't going to fall and break his neck. If he did fall and injured himself, that would be it. His career would be over—there'd be no trials, no Olympics, and he'd have a foolproof excuse to quit gymnastics forever. Then again, without gymnastics, what did he really have? He couldn't even begin to think what he might do without it. The thought filled his chest, tightening unexpectedly, and he glanced at the ropes. It would be so easy to just let himself fall.

"Come on," Shane called from the ground, his *safe* place on the ground, "The big strong gymnast can't be scared of a few rocks."

The strain was unexpected in his arms as Auden clung to the wall, sucking in air and reminding himself that he did more dangerous stunts on a daily basis with no ropes to catch him in case he fell. He'd never done anything like this—gymnastics was certainly never this terrifying. The scariest part of gymnastics lately was the idea of the impending trials that would determine his fate.

If he fell and was injured, he'd have to find something else to do, and aside from playing too many video games in his off hours, he wasn't sure he knew what he would do. He supposed he'd go to college, somewhere farther away from his parents so they couldn't drop in unannounced. He'd be able to have a life. He'd have normal friends. He could study oceanography or architecture or... something. He could study whatever he wanted.

He just had to make it up the wall, he told himself firmly, reaching for the next handhold and hoisting himself up.

"Use your legs," Shane called from below.

Auden was sure he was using muscles he didn't even have, and he hoped to God that he wouldn't regret this tomorrow. Dorian would murder him if he came in sore from an un-gymnastics-related activity. He climbed slowly up the wall, stopping near the top. He didn't dare look down and consider how far he had to fall.

"Okay, can I come down now?"

Shane grinned and tightened the belay again. "Slowly."

Feeling relieved, he climbed back to the ground as slowly as possible. At the bottom, Shane unhooked the belay rope, and Auden was grateful to be back on solid ground.

"It's not that bad," Shane assured him. "This is just the trial run anyway."

"For the real stuff," Auden finished, though it didn't sound too appealing.

"Part of the fun is being terrified. Can't be afraid to take a chance," Shane said easily, reaching up and squeezing the back of Auden's neck. Auden froze at the touch, friendly and easy. It was so unexpected, so different than Trayce's touch. "Wasn't it a rush up there?"

"It was definitely something." Auden didn't know quite what it had been. He could still feel the shaking nerves in his fingers, the lingering fear that had followed him up. Considering how much time he spent doing dangerous stunts that could get himself killed, gymnastics had never made him feel like that. Being on the rock, even if it was only a fake wall made of plastic hand and footholds, had only made him nervous, like anything could go wrong at any second. The more he thought about it, though, the more he had to agree with Shane. "Yeah. It kind of was."

Shane grinned and dropped his hand from Auden's neck. "We'll make an outdoorsman of you yet. I can't believe you've been in Phoenix so long and you've never done any of this stuff."

"I don't really get out that much." The most Auden saw of the city was Mill Avenue and occasionally one of the many malls that Anya dragged him to on their days off.

"You definitely should. There's more than just cement and shopping malls around here." They started towards the exit, Shane opening the door for Auden. "I'm betting you've never been on the Salt River?"

"There's a river with water in it?" Auden asked skeptically. Of all the 'rivers' he'd ever seen in Arizona, none had actually had water in them.

"Yeah," Shane said, laughing. He pushed open the front door to the parking lot and a blast of hot air hit them in the face. "In late summer, it's a great place to go tubing. Grab some beers and float down the river. You should come."

Late summer was months from then, an entire lifetime away, but Auden nodded. "Sure." As they walked to the car, he glanced over at Shane.

Shane, although not terribly tall, was good-looking by most standards, good-looking in a way that should have made Auden think about closed doors and groping hands, but whenever his mind went there, Shane's dark curls morphed into Trayce's short black hair. Shane's smooth complexion faded into scattered freckles, skin a shade lighter, straight nose becoming crooked in his mind. It wasn't something he could get out of his head no matter how hard he tried. Thoughts of Shane biting at his skin became memories of Trayce doing the same.

"Want to get some coffee?" Shane asked as they reached Shane's car. At Auden's pause, he added, "or tea, water, whatever."

"Sure." Auden opened the door, stepping back to let the heat seep out, blistering in the sun. He really shouldn't have been out since he'd spent the whole morning running drills, and hauling himself up that rock wall had left every muscle protesting. Dorian would be pissed if he came to training tomorrow with any muscle problems. Maybe after he got back, he should go see the team physical therapist.

They drove to a café Auden had never been to before, somewhere out of the way. Inside, it was nice and cool, the smell of coffee and pastries wafting through the air. A few people sat at tables near the window and Shane picked one out of the way.

"This is nice," Auden said, feeling awkward again as they sat there. It was easy for this to become awkward, for the silences to be a little longer than necessary. It wouldn't have been like this with Trayce. They would have been talking about trials or skills. Not that Auden wanted to talk about that right now, but at least with Trayce, they would have something to say.

"Better than the mainstream coffee chains that charge an arm and a leg for a cup full of sugar," Shane offered, crossing his arms on the table and gazing at Auden. "Would you go rock climbing again?"

"Yeah," Auden said after a moment. "Once you get over the life-threatening part, it was kind of fun."

"It's freeing," Shane supplied. "I mean, sure, there's the possibility of death if you fall and the rope breaks, but that's part of the thrill. You must love the thrill of sports, right? Gymnastics is just one step away from injury every time, right?"

"It's not exactly the same," Auden admitted. "I've trained for a long time so that won't happen."

"But you can't predict everything."

"I guess." Auden had to admit that. He'd been injured a lot when he was younger, but what gymnast hadn't? It was part of what made the sport a challenge. "I just have to make it through the next few months."

"Didn't you say something about trials?" Shane picked through the sugar packets on the table, not meeting Auden's gaze as Auden sighed.

"About a month." Auden nodded, his stomach knotting at the thought. "I don't know what I'm going to do."

"What do you mean?"

Auden hesitated, tearing his napkin into pieces and glancing out the window at a woman who'd obviously had too much plastic surgery walk past with a small, conspicuously-groomed dog. He shook his head instead. "I don't know. It's just a lot of pressure."

He wasn't even sure if he wanted to do the trials. It wasn't as easy as just saying so, though. Saying it would make it real—would mean that maybe he didn't want to be a gymnast anymore. He couldn't bring himself to admit that.

"If it were me, I wouldn't waste the time. There are better things to do." Shane tore open the sugar packet and it spilled on the table. He swept it away with as much delicacy as his last sentence.

Auden didn't have a response for that. He'd spent every minute of the last ten years working towards one thing. 'Better' hadn't been a thought. What could have been better than gymnastics? He didn't like to think that he'd wasted the last ten years either. If he'd said that to his parents, his dad would probably have a heart attack.

"I guess I'm just trying to figure it out."

Shane nodded slowly. "Well, lucky for you, you've got me now and I can show you all the other things that are out there."

"Like what?" Auden wasn't sure he even knew what else there

was to do. Something that didn't injure him every time he tried a new skill? Something that didn't require thirty hours of training every week? Something that didn't make him feel like crawling into a corner whenever someone mentioned competition? Maybe there was something else out there.

"You like music, right? You like rock climbing now." Shane grinned. "There are millions of other things to do in the world aside from jump around on a mat." He rolled his eyes.

Gymnastics was much more than that, Auden thought, almost insulted for a moment, but he didn't argue right then, not when Shane's foot slid against his leg.

"I guess," he agreed instead, shifting in his chair and meeting Shane's grin. It would have been so easy to lean across the table and kiss him, and as he sat there, he wondered what was holding him back. Here was Shane, a nice guy who had interests that didn't include tunnel vision, and yet Auden hesitated. He probably could have invited Shane to the bathroom in that café and he would have come. It would have been easy to do, easy to say, easy to drop to his knees and suck him off right there.

As much as he wanted to, though, he couldn't bring himself to say it. Instead, he watched Shane and felt the slide of his foot against his inseam. He didn't stop Shane but he didn't encourage it either. For a second, he thought of Trayce, of Trayce sitting across from him with the same look in his eye as Shane had. A thrill rippled through his stomach and he bit his tongue. This would never happen with Trayce, though, and he needed to get a grip, he told himself firmly. Shane wasn't Trayce and Trayce would never be Shane.

Auden wasn't sure what he was doing, but he pushed his chair back and stood, hesitating for a second. "I'm gonna go wash my hands," he said slowly, glancing at Shane but then heading for the small bathroom in the back of the café.

The bathroom was small with flowered wallpaper bordering the top. At the sink, Auden didn't wash his hands but waited. Maybe Shane hadn't gotten the message. Maybe he should have been more explicit, but Auden wasn't very good at this sort of thing. He jumped when the doorknob rattled, but Shane stepped in, locking the door behind him.

"Subtle," Shane said, smiling slightly as he backed Auden up against the sink. "Didn't peg you for the public sex type. Thought you'd be all flowers and candles for the first time."

"Would you have?" Auden asked, nerves rising in his throat because what Shane said was true. It hadn't been like that with Trayce and Trayce would never have even considered it.

"I don't have flowers but I'm sure I could find candles somewhere," Shane replied. "If that's what you want."

Trayce would have said that Auden was far too much of a romantic for anyone to handle. Auden took a step back, the sink digging into his lower back, and he hesitated.

"We could go back to my place," Shane offered, leaning in to Auden's neck, his fingers brushing up his arm, raising goosebumps along the skin. "Find some candles, take off our clothes, get rid of this awkwardness that's following us around. You are really toned," he murmured. "And I'd like to see more of you."

Auden's eyes fluttered shut for a second as Shane pressed a kiss to his jaw. It was different than anything with Trayce had ever been. The moments were slower, a drag against his mind, imprinting there for later.

"Or," Shane went on, hands sliding over Auden's torso and dragging against his shirt. "We could get a good story out of this bathroom thing."

Auden laughed despite his nerves. He wanted to prove to Shane that he was interested, prove to himself that he could forget about Trayce for more than a minute, and that, perhaps, was what made him step forward, pushing Shane back against the door.

"Let's make a story," he said, sliding to his knees.

"I like that idea," Shane breathed above him, a hand stroking through his hair.

On the hard tile floor, Auden reached for Shane's shorts and pulled them down easily, fabric gliding over his hips. It wasn't as though he'd never done this before, but it was usually with Trayce who didn't make him feel nervous, worried about how it might go. Pushing those thoughts aside, he peeled down Shane's underwear, revealing his soft cock underneath. It looked different than he'd expected, smaller than Trayce's but longer. Leaning in, his pressed his mouth to Shane's thigh, sliding his hand up to grip his dick and stroke slowly.

They had to be quick, he knew, but he didn't want this to be rushed. He wanted Shane to enjoy it. Moving a bit faster, though, he stroked Shane until Shane's cock began to harden in his hand and he heard Shane's soft exhale above him.

"You're not half bad," Shane breathed, and Auden heard the smile in his voice.

He didn't want to be 'half-bad,' though, and he moved up, sliding his mouth from Shane's thigh to the tip of his cock, sucking it into his mouth and flicking his tongue over it. His grip tightened and then relaxed, jerking Shane off as he moved in. He took Shane into his mouth, sliding his tongue over his prick and sucking until Shane was cursing above him, a hand digging into his shoulder and hips making jerky movements.

"Oh shit, oh shit," Shane gasped, but Auden didn't slow down. He was all too aware of the time that had already passed since they'd entered the bathroom. He wanted Shane to come, to come hard like he just couldn't control himself.

Spreading Shane's legs, he sucked his cock harder, adjusting the pressure on his knees. Shane's prick was hot and heavy in his mouth, a bitter taste on his tongue, different than Trayce. Before he could stop himself, his mind flitted to Trayce, Trayce sucking him off, bright eyes watching him every moment until he came. Auden was starting to get hard, but he shook himself, shaking away Trayce's face in his mind.

Shane's hand tightened on Auden's shoulder, and it was the only warning he got before Shane came. Pulling away, he wiped his mouth and jerked Shane through his shuddering orgasm.

"Fuck," Shane muttered, sighing loudly and reaching for a paper towel to clean up. Auden climbed to his feet, feeling shaky, a mixture of pleased and confused at his own brain. Why couldn't he just forget about Trayce for even a minute? "Definitely a good memory."

Auden smiled as he washed his hands and was surprised when Shane wrapped his arms around him from the back and pressed a kiss to the side of his neck.

"Not how I pictured it, but you surprised me."

"That a good thing?"

Shane grinned and kissed his neck again. "Surprises are always good things."

Auden tossed away the paper towel and smiled back at him. "I guess so."

Chapter 9

Unusually Late

Auden felt all eyes on him as he entered the gym, and he knew exactly why. The clock read seven-twenty, twenty minutes after he was supposed to have been there. As he passed by Trayce, he avoided his gaze. Somehow, he felt guilty, a gnawing sensation deep in his chest that was associated with Trayce.

It had to do with Shane too, and how he'd spent most of last night at Shane's apartment. They'd spent it watching movies, staying up too late.

"You can't tell me you've never seen Ghostbusters?*" Shane said, sitting close enough so that his knee touched Auden's.*

"That movie is ancient. My parents watched it when they were growing up. It was made, like, forty years ago." Most of the movies Auden watched were old Superhero movies that came out when he was in middle school and high school. He'd watched Black Widow *a thousand times, but he'd never really been into comedies.*

"It's the remake, with Melissa McCarthy. How about this one; it's a documentary on the 2018 Olympics, when the US ski champion fell headfirst on his jump and was paralyzed," Shane said, reading the description off the screen, flipping through the movie choices.

Auden grimaced. "The Olympics are not something I want to think about, especially not one where people get injured."

"I hate sports movies anyway," Shane said, tossing the remote aside, his hand falling on Auden's knee. "The other day, I climbed up to the top of the mountain and spent the whole day meditating. It was really freeing."

Auden smiled. He wasn't sure meditating was something he would ever be good at it. He'd tried it a few times, but every time, he just got dis-

tracted by thoughts of training, or else Anya would burst in and interrupt.
"I'm not that great at it."

Shane brushed back his hair gently and smiled. "You just need to forget about these stupid Olympics."

Auden sighed as he crossed the gym, trying to ignore everyone's gaze. It was becoming so easy to be with Shane, though, to spend time with him without any pressure. Of course, that meant facing the consequences when he let it interfere with training. He hadn't meant for it to. It had been an accident.

Dorian stood at the end of the gym, arms crossed over his chest, and he didn't say a word as Auden approached him. Being late was simply not permitted at the Center, and Auden knew that full well.

"Auden," Dorian said as he reached him. "Nice of you to show up."

"Sorry, Coach. My alarm, I didn't hear it, I—"

Dorian cleared his throat and Auden stopped abruptly. He was about to be in big trouble, he just knew it. The last person who was late to practice had gotten chewed out for an entire half an hour and then was sent to run laps in the eighty degree morning.

"Get with Coach Spencer and start your warm-ups," Dorian said sharply, surprising Auden.

"Yes, okay," he said slowly, but he didn't feel reassured by the steely glint in Dorian's eye as he turned to find the assistant coach. He still felt everyone's eyes on him as he crossed the gym, but after a moment, they went back to warm-ups.

Settling into his warm-ups, Auden still felt uneasy. He'd never, not once in his entire career, been late to practice. He'd woken up this morning to his clock telling him he only had ten minutes to get to the gym. He'd barely had time to get dressed let alone do anything else. Dorian's reaction hadn't reassured him either. When Dorian was calm, it could only mean bad things.

No one spoke to him all through warm-ups, however, not until they'd broken off to work on skills.

"What the hell is going on?" Trayce asked as they waited by the mat for Liam to finish his routine.

"What do you mean?" Auden rolled his shoulders, not looking at Trayce.

"What do you think I mean?" Trayce asked, shaking his head. "You were late. You're never late."

"I just didn't hear my alarm."

"Bullshit. It's not just that," Trayce said, turning towards Auden. "You've been acting weird for a while."

"Well, it's none of your business if I have," Auden replied, sighing. "I can do what I want, Trayce. You don't get a say in my life."

Trayce paused, and Auden glanced at him finally to find him looking insulted and slightly pissed off.

"Sorry, I thought we were friends, which somehow equated to me being able to have an opinion."

Auden didn't know what to say, and he frowned. He wasn't upset with Trayce, necessarily, but he couldn't explain it. Trayce only had opinions when it came to training. He didn't care about any other aspect of his life. They weren't boyfriends, as Trayce had pointed out many times before. They didn't have to pretend to be anything more than friends.

"I'm just tired," he said finally, though he knew it wasn't the best excuse he could come up with.

"Tired of what?" Trayce asked, staring at him, as though daring him to answer. "That's the real question, isn't it, Auden?"

Auden didn't have an answer for him, and he was saved answering as Dorian came over.

"Auden, let's talk," he said abruptly in a way that gave no room for questioning. Auden wasn't sure who he'd rather talk to at this point, but he didn't have a choice as Dorian led him away from the mat and Trayce. "How've you been feeling lately?" Dorian asked as they walked out of the gym and down the hallway towards his office.

"Fine," Auden lied, such an automatic response at this point that he almost believed it.

"In all the time I've coached you, you've never been late once. You've never skipped a practice or stopped for anything. You've been one of the most dedicated athletes I've seen come through here. This year's batch have the most potential to make it to the Olympics that I've ever seen, and I'd hate to see you let it go to waste."

"It was just my alarm—"

"Didn't go off," Dorian finished for him. He paused in front of a picture in the hall. "When I was your age, I'd already been to the Olympics. I'd seen my dream come and go and I was left with an injury that made getting up in the morning the hardest thing to do. You're lucky you haven't been injured yet, you know that."

Auden nodded. He did know that—he was lucky to be in such good shape after so many years of training and competing. He was lucky that he had a shot at the Olympics and good odds that he would actually make the team, but he still couldn't bring himself to feel anything other than dread when he thought about it.

Dorian gazed at Auden for a long moment and then glanced back at the photo. It was the one of the 2008 Olympic team with Jules and Dorian in middle. "It isn't easy to lose something you've been working towards for so long but it's even harder to lose it before you even have it." He turned to Auden. "I know it's a lot of pressure, and I know it isn't easy to want something you may not get, but that doesn't mean you give up before you try."

"I'm not giving up, I..." Auden didn't even know what he was arguing.

Dorian patted his shoulder. "I understand what you're feeling, but if you're late again, you'll be running drills from morning till night. Got it?"

Auden nodded quickly, glad Dorian hadn't decided to chew him out. He almost would have felt better if he had, though. At least then, he could feel annoyed instead of even more guilty at Dorian's support.

"Now get back in there and you better work twice as hard."

"Sure, Coach," Auden replied, heading back to the gym. He wished he could just forget about everything for one minute, but life never seemed to work out that way.

"I heard you were late to practice," Anya said as she picked at her salad and pushed it away with a face. "Did Dorian rip you a new one?"

"No." Auden sighed. It would have been easier if he had. "He just talked about pressure and trials. The usual."

"You do need to be careful," Anya reminded him seriously. "If Dorian thinks you're not serious, he could recommend you not compete."

Auden didn't say he'd be glad if he did. Instead, he unscrewed his water bottle and took a sip. The cafeteria around them was full of other athletes, but Trayce hadn't shown up yet, for which Auden was glad. He didn't have an answer to his question still.

"It was just a mistake. I was late one time. It's not like I skipped training entirely or came in hungover. It's not a huge deal."

"Of course it is!" She stared at him. "You're so close to trials. You can't afford to slip up now!"

Auden rolled his eyes but didn't reply. There was nothing he could say that she would believe anyway.

Anya frowned and grabbed the orange on her plate. Peeling it slowly, she glanced at him carefully.

"You're okay, right?"

"I'm fine," Auden replied for the millionth time. "It was just one time. I wish everyone would stop making such a big deal out of it."

Anya shrugged evasively. "Okay, fine. You're fine. Whatever. So where's Trayce?"

"How should I know?" Auden purposefully didn't glance around the cafeteria. He didn't want to find Trayce. He would just make things more complicated.

"He's pretty much your only friend other than me," Anya pointed out. "And he's not really friendly with the other guys on the team so when he's not here, I figure you know why."

"Well, I don't." Auden had no idea where Trayce was nor did he care to find out. "Haven't seen him since this morning."

"Did you have a fight?"

Auden shot her a look at the question. "No."

Anya waved her fork at him. "Someday one of you is going to realize that your little friends-with-benefits arrangement is really just code for boyfriends."

"It is not."

"Is," she replied bluntly. "It'd be a lot easier if you'd both just admit it."

"Trayce doesn't want that," Auden muttered instead, pushing at his food, but it looked entirely unappetizing. "He thinks relationships are stupid and pointless and everyone just gets hurt in the end."

Anya scoffed. "Imagine that."

"What's that supposed to mean?"

"Well, someone is definitely going to get hurt here. I just hope it's not you."

Auden frowned. "We're just—"

"Friends." Anya rolled her eyes. "I know."

Auden didn't even know what the point was in lying anymore.

Auden went running down the mat, a backflip and double salto as he bounced into the corner. Dorian watched from the sideline, hands on his hips and mouth set in a tight line. The next skill was the new one, and Auden took a breath as he stepped into the corner and took off. The first jump went smoothly, but the twist was all wrong as he came into the second one and he smashed down, the mat hurtling up into his knee.

Searing pain shot through him as he collapsed, gasping for breath as his vision went cloudy with pain. Clutching his knee, he rolled over, squeezing his eyes shut against the feeling of knives piercing his skin.

"Auden," came Dorian's voice from somewhere above him. "Auden, just relax. One injury isn't the end of the world."

Auden could do nothing but clutch at his knee, in too much pain to move, but he opened his eyes at Trayce's voice that seemed to echo.

"You can't compete in the trials anymore," he said, glancing at Auden's swollen knee. "Don't worry. I'll fill your spot just fine."

Auden stared up, his heart sinking as Trayce laughed. The laughing filled the gym, bouncing off the walls, bombarding his ears, and Auden pressed his palms to his ears, trying to block it out. This couldn't be the end.

Auden woke with a start in the pitch black dorm room. Immediately, he reached for his knee to find it perfectly intact. Letting out a breath, he pushed himself up. For a moment, he thought it had been real. If it had been real, he would have been out of the competition for good. As he sat there in the dark, he wasn't sure what made him feel better — the thought that it had been a dream or that it hadn't.

He sighed, lying back down and staring at the ceiling. He should have been relieved that it had only been a dream, but a part of him wasn't sure he was.

Chapter 10
Just a Friend

Trials loomed ever closer on the horizon ("Thirty-two days!" Anya piped up brightly that morning). Auden wasn't sure how she could be excited when she couldn't even compete. Last he'd heard, her physical therapist had suggested she take a year off from training. She never would, though. If she had her way, she'd be back in the gym by the end of the summer.

Auden, on the other hand, had decided that the only way he was going to get through this was by spending as much time away from the gym as possible. He avoided Trayce's gaze whenever they had to be together, and he just knew Trayce was waiting for an opportunity to ask him too many questions again, to push until Auden gave up and admitted that he didn't know what the hell he wanted anymore.

As much as he had hoped that Shane might make things less complicated, Auden found that it was just the opposite. Shane was fun and interesting and he didn't talk about gymnastics. Instead, they spent their time hiking and rock climbing (Auden was getting much better at the wall), and Shane had even taught him a few chords on the guitar. Spending time with him was a complete turnaround from how it was with Trayce.

"Look, it's easy," Shane said, reaching over and adjusting Auden's fingers on the guitar. "Just a little further with this one and you've got an A minor chord."

"Is A minor crucial to playing music?"

"Punk music, yes. All the minor chords are very important," Shane replied seriously and then grinned at Auden. He moved to sit next to him on the couch and took the guitar from him. "You're a pretty quick learner."

"It comes from being competitive," Auden admitted. "Always have to be the best, you know."

"I'm not really like that," Shane said, strumming a few chords. "I figure whatever's gonna happen is gonna happen. Have you been working on your meditation?"

"Not really." Auden grimaced. He hadn't even really thought about it since that first date on the mountain. It just didn't seem like something important to do, not when he had so many other things to worry about.

"It's good for your soul," Shane said. "Helps you have a clearer head."

Auden laughed slightly. "That would be nice."

"We can work on it." Shane smiled. He set the guitar on the coffee table and pulled Auden's feet into his lap. Auden let him. It had gotten easier, this part, being with Shane. He could almost do it completely without thinking of Trayce. "So if you're so competitive, how come it doesn't feel like it?"

Auden shrugged. "I try not to be a jerk about it like some people can be. I'm competitive but I want other people to do well too."

"So you're a nice competitive, not a jerk competitive."

"Yeah."

"And you're the best?"

Auden hesitated. "I don't know. Everyone says so but I kind of wish I wasn't. At least then I could have a life outside of gymnastics."

Shane nodded, his hand resting on Auden's ankle, thumb brushing over his skin softly. "You do now. You don't need to bother with gymnastics anymore."

Auden didn't completely agree, and he frowned slightly at Shane's words. What did that mean exactly? He did at least have somewhere to go other than the gym, somewhere he could escape to when the pressure got too much, but he couldn't give up completely. Glancing at Shane, he hesitated, something nagging at the back of his mind, but he pushed it away as he leaned over and kissed Shane.

It still felt different than with Trayce, not entirely easy yet, but Shane moved with him easily, letting Auden settle on top. Auden closed his eyes as they kissed, sliding his hands into Shane's hair and sucking on his bottom lip. Shane's hands came up to rest on his hips and Shane spread his legs for Auden to sink between them.

This part was easy, getting lost in the feeling of Shane — the taste, the touch. It was easy to fall into him, mouths moving together slowly but purposefully. It wasn't messy or rushed like it usually was with Trayce. Shane moved against him, pushing his hips up, his erection grinding into Auden's.

Shane moaned softly against his mouth, and his hands pushed under Auden's shirt, skimming it up to his shoulders. He broke the kiss to get it off, tossing it somewhere behind the couch. His mouth ghosted over Auden's and Auden felt the familiar flutter deep in his chest, one he usually only got with Trayce, but here it was with Shane staring at him, dark brown eyes locked on his. He felt nervous all of a sudden, unsure of himself, but Shane's hands went for his jeans a moment later and he reminded himself that he knew what he was doing.

All those times with Trayce had at least prepared him for this moment with someone else. He could slip out of his jeans, could reach down and get Shane out of his as well. Soon, they were both naked, hands exploring as mouths met, tongues sliding together, the soft press of lips against skin. Auden gasped at Shane's hands on his body, sliding down to grip his ass, to grind their hips together until they were both panting, hard and sweaty.

"Shane," Auden breathed as he pulled away to catch his breath, his cock as hard as it had ever been. "Do you have —"

Shane didn't reply but stretched back for the table near the couch. He rummaged for a moment and came up with a condom. The wrapper was faded as though it had been there for a while.

"For emergencies." Shane smirked against Auden's mouth.

Shane didn't kiss him again, instead pressing his mouth to Auden's chest, sliding down to mouth along his hip bone as Auden stretched above him, heat flooding his cock. He sucked in a sharp breath as Shane pressed his palm into the hard length in his boxers before moving down to mouth at his erection.

Licking his lips, Auden breathed out slowly, closing his eyes against the warmth, the pressure around his prick as Shane stroked him through the fabric. Shane glanced up, eyes locking with Auden's as Auden looked down.

Neither said anything, and Auden let his head fall back against the pillow as Shane hooked his fingers under the waist of his boxers and pulled.

Auden squeezed his eyes shut for a second as his hips lifted off the bed. He didn't want to see Shane's reaction. He just wanted to feel it.

He got his wish a second later as Shane's mouth pressed against his cock, licking up the underside, but he didn't take him in his mouth, instead sitting up, and Auden heard the rustle of fabric — Shane's boxers being shed to the floor.

Shane stretched back up Auden's body, taking his time tracing each muscle with his tongue until Auden was practically a puddle in his hands, every nerve-ending on fire as Shane's mouth moved up his stomach to his chest, teeth closing around a nipple and sucking as Auden groaned.

Auden's hand slid into Shane's curls for the first time, stroking down a ringlet and watching it spring back when he let it go. He smiled but interrupted it to gasp as Shane moved to his neck, licking the dip between his collarbone and neck.

"God," he breathed, licking his lips and letting his eyes close against the press of Shane's mouth, the glide of his hands over his stomach, the press of their hips, Shane's cock rocking against his. Reaching down, he let hands wander over Shane's chest.

"I'm not nearly as ripped as the guys you normally see," Shane said, pushing a curl from his eyes and Auden laughed, though his mind automatically went to Trayce, how Trayce's body felt under his hands.

"It's okay," he replied, shifting beneath him, feeling the hot press of Shane's cock against his.

"Just how flexible are you?" Shane asked curiously after a second, and Auden smiled, drawing his knees up.

"How flexible do you want me to be?"

Shane paused and then grinned, an eyebrow arching up as he eyed Auden. He slid his hands down Auden's thighs, pushing his legs up, past his head, and Auden didn't even flinch. This was nothing. He could go further.

"This'll do."

Auden's mouth twitched into a smile, but he couldn't shake the feeling that something wasn't quite right. It felt different, different than with Trayce. It wasn't just the way Shane's fingers pushed inside him, slick with lube, the way he slid his hips in, his cock pressing through Auden's muscles. Auden sucked in a sharp breath at the pressure, the flush creeping over his skin. It was in the way Shane reached for his face, drawing his chin up to kiss him deeply, tongue sweeping inside his mouth. Trayce never did that.

Auden shook himself sharply. He shouldn't have been thinking about Trayce at a time like this, not with Shane's cock pressed inside his body, filling him until he could only choke on his breath and came in sharp pants.

Shane moved slowly at first, building up a steady rhythm that had the couch legs edging back and forth along the floor, the dull scrape of each thrust echoing around them. Shane's arms kept Auden's legs up as he rocked in, back and forth, an easy push as they both breathed heavily.

Auden's hands curled around Shane's side, digging in as he bit his lip and panted for breath, feeling Shane's face close to his, feeling the puff of hot air on his cheek as Shane moved, pushing in faster now. He only had to turn his mouth slightly to find Shane's, their lips sliding together, Shane pulling at his bottom lip with his teeth as Auden moaned softly.

Shane reached for Auden's cock finally, and Auden squeezed his eyes shut against the pressure that spiked as he did so. Shane's nose bumped against Auden's as he stroked him, hips pushing in harder.

Shane didn't tease him like Trayce would have. Instead, he increased his speed, jerking him off until Auden gasped, his fingers digging into Shane's side as his release snapped inside him, a sharp desperation as he came, sticky and wet on his stomach.

"Fuck," Shane cursed as he pushed in harder, faster.

Auden sighed long and slow as he watched Shane push in, felt the hard thrust deep inside him, the couch scraping against the floor. He watched Shane bow his head, curls falling over his eyes.

He could see the way his mouth fell open as he pushed in one more time and groaned loudly.

"Jesus Christ," Shane breathed a minute later as his hips slowed and he sighed, shaking his hair from his eyes.

Auden's legs slipped down and he took a moment to gather himself. It certainly wasn't what he was used to—somehow softer and harder at the same time. With Shane draped over him, he wasn't quite sure what to do, but Shane pushed himself up a minute later, hovering over Auden.

"That guy you've been sort of seeing," he said finally, and Auden felt his stomach recoil uneasily. "Think maybe it's time you broke it off?"

For a second, Auden hesitated, swallowing down the lump rising in his throat. He wasn't sure how Trayce would take it—in fact, he wasn't sure he could even bring himself to do it, but Shane gazed at him unwaveringly and he couldn't say no. Besides, Shane was the one that wanted to be with him, not Trayce. It would be a good thing, he tried to convince himself.

In the end, he nodded jerkily but as Shane brushed a kiss against his lips, he couldn't shake the unsettled feeling in his chest.

The routine came too easy—too boring. Every move was followed swiftly by another, every element linked together smoothly, and Auden wasn't sure he even had to think about it anymore, and that was when it all fell apart. Landing on the mat, he stumbled back, losing his footing and barely catching himself from crashing into the floor. On his hands and knees, he took a deep breath and closed his eyes against the bright blue of the mat underneath him.

"Auden!" Dorian's voice snapped close by and Auden forced his eyes open and climbed to his feet. Dorian had come onto the mat and seemed to be giving him a once-over. "You okay?"

"Fine." Auden dusted himself off. He needed to get a grip. It was one thing to dream about injuring himself but it was another thing entirely to actually do it.

Dorian crossed his arms, though, at his answer, the corners of his mouth tugging into a frown. "You've been off."

"Just tired, I guess."

Dorian shook his head. "Not just today." He paused, but he must have decided not to push because he dropped his arms and nodded at the mat. "Watch over-rotating the pike. If you get ahead of yourself, you'll end up on your ass as you just discovered. Now's not the time to get complacent, Auden."

"Yeah, Coach," Auden replied, rolling out his shoulders and stepping up to the mat again.

Even faced with the floor, Auden's mind still wasn't on it. The worst thing a gymnast could do was lose concentration during a skill—it could lead to mistakes, or worse, injuries. Still, his mind was somewhere else as he started his routine over again. It was back in Shane's apartment, listening to Shane's words, feeling Shane's hands on his skin.

He made the first element easily, but as he turned, he caught sight of Trayce across the gym. Trayce was working on his rings routine for the hundredth time, the assistant coach barking things at him from beneath. Auden still hadn't really talked to Trayce since the other day and their disagreement. He couldn't avoid him forever, though, and a part of Auden just wanted to get the confrontation over with. Besides, he had to tell Trayce it was over.

The thought of breaking things off with Trayce made his chest tighten uncomfortably and he tried to push it aside in favor of focusing on his triple salto, but he barely made a double before the feeling came rushing back along with a flinch of disappointment as Dorian barked at him a second later.

"Auden, what the hell was that?"

Auden sighed and grabbed a towel off the bench. He didn't have an explanation that Dorian would accept.

Dorian frowned so severely that Auden wondered if his face might actually stay like that permanently. It certainly wasn't a reassuring look. He wished Jules was around to loosen him up, but he hadn't seen Jules in a while. He was probably on one of his announcing stints.

"I'm trying to be understanding," Dorian said slowly. "But you have to work with me here. I'm not here to waste my time and I hope you aren't either. Trials are less than a month away and I can see you slipping."

Auden took a breath but said nothing. He wasn't sure what he would say anyway. Would he just tell Dorian that he wasn't sure he even wanted to go to trials anymore? Would he say that gymnastics had become pointless? He had spent so much time working towards one single moment, and what if he didn't make it? Everyone would be disappointed in him. And if he did make it, they would expect him to win. They would expect him to get the gold and then what? Then nothing. He didn't get money or fame, at least not much and not for very long. It wasn't like other sports.

Dorian stepped closer and lowered his voice. "I never told anyone, but I was scared shitless my first time at trials."

"But you were amazing."

He shrugged. "Doesn't make a difference how talented you are. Everyone is scared. The point is to do it anyway."

"I'm not scared," Auden said simply, and when Dorian merely arched an eyebrow, he frowned. "I'm not." That wasn't why he didn't want to compete. It wasn't.

"Go warm up for the horse," Dorian said instead, giving his shoulder a shove towards the pommel horse, "but don't think you've gotten out of this routine. If I catch you messing up again, you'll be doing those jumps in your sleep."

Auden left him and moved over to the pommel horse, smoothing his hand over the firm fabric, covered in chalk.

"You just gonna hand me the gold medal or what?" Trayce asked abruptly from behind Auden.

Auden's heart jumped into his throat but he forced himself to turn, to act normally. He had to tell Trayce that he was breaking it off, but as he faced him, he wasn't sure he could do it. Standing behind him, Trayce had his arms crossed, a glisten of sweat along his brow, chest moving up and down quickly like he'd jumped off the rings just so he could come over and insult Auden. Come to think of it, he probably had.

"If you want it that badly," Auden replied, not flinching when Trayce stepped closer, eyes flicking over him, searching for something though Auden wasn't sure what.

"Don't you want it that badly?" Trayce asked, tilting his head to the side. "Or has this new guy of yours convinced you to give up everything you love for a fuck on the side?"

Auden frowned. "That's not what—"

"I saw him drop you off the other night," Trayce interrupted. "I saw that disgusting display of affection in front of the dorms." He made a face but kept a close watch on Auden as he said it.

"If it was so disgusting, why did you watch?" Sometimes Auden didn't understand Trayce. He could go from friendly and playful to sharp and sarcastic at the drop of a hat.

Trayce shrugged, though he looked away from Auden, across the gym instead. "Curiosity."

Shaking his head, Auden rolled his eyes. "Shane has nothing to do with my training."

"Please," Trayce scoffed. "He's the reason you've been shit at all your events lately. It's like you just want to give away your spot on the Olympic team."

"Look, I told you about him," Auden said, lowering his voice so no one would hear them arguing. "You didn't care. I don't know why you do now."

"I care because you're fucking up your chances at accomplishing a lifelong goal over some prick."

"Shane is not a prick."

"Whatever. I don't care what he is. I just care what he's doing."

"He's paying attention to me," Auden snapped. "It's more than you do."

Trayce paused, staring at Auden, then taking a step back. "I'm not your boyfriend, Auden."

"Sometimes I'm not even sure you're my friend."

For a second, something other than anger flickered in Trayce's eyes, but it was gone before Auden could tell what it was. Maybe he'd gone too far. Trayce's shoulders stiffened along with the tightening in his jaw.

"Tell your *friend* he can go fuck himself," Trayce said finally, turning and walking away before Auden could say anything else.

Chapter 11
Exploring Options

The record store was dead except for a few teenagers huddled in a corner gaping at an amp. Auden browsed the new releases, but there wasn't anything he didn't already have, nothing new since the last time he'd come. He'd just needed to get away from everything, and the record store had always felt comfortable.

The store was a hole-in-the-wall place off Mill Avenue, usually dimly lit, speakers playing whatever punk-indie-pop-rock mix the owner wanted. Today, it was My Chemical Romance, a classic, Shane would have said, but an oldie nonetheless. Sunlight filtered in through the front window, but the further back it got, the darker it became, casting shadows over the dusty CDs that hardly anyone bought anymore. Auden just liked the physicality of an actual CD, even if he could hardly find a player to save his life these days.

Turning from the albums, he scanned the walls of the shop, hung with guitars for sale. He spotted one Shane had showed him a photo of—a jet black Fender double neck Strat. There had only been a handful made and Auden grimaced at the price. It was definitely out of his range.

"You have good taste," Oscar said from behind Auden.

Oscar owned the place. A Hispanic man in his late thirties, he said he wanted to keep the tradition of music alive with real CDs and records. So far, his store was the only one Auden had found in Phoenix with a real variety.

Auden smiled slightly. "My friend told me about that one."

Oscar nodded. "One of only two hundred. They were only made for the Japanese market, so it's lucky we've got one."

Auden couldn't even imagine paying five thousand dollars for a guitar. As much as he liked music, it just seemed astronomical. Then again, his parents paid that much for four months of training at the Center. Some people might have thought that was a lot. As much as his dad complained about the cost, Auden knew he wouldn't have kept paying if he wasn't sure his money was being spent wisely.

The thought made Auden uneasy. Even his dad, who would rather he wasn't spending so much of his money, thought it was worth it.

"You want to have a go?" Oscar asked as they stood there, and Auden's eyes widened.

"On that? No, no, I couldn't—"

"Sure you can!" Oscar grabbed a stool and took the Fender off the wall carefully. "Just be gentle, okay?"

Auden wasn't so sure this was a good idea. He'd only ever held a guitar a few times in his life, and never one so expensive. Shane's guitar was much easier, much less pressure. Auden took the guitar from Oscar, though, and held it around the neck as though it might bite him.

Oscar laughed. "It's not a snake. Here." He reached for the guitar and tipped it into Auden's grip the right way. He stepped back, nodding, satisfied. "It suits you."

Auden wasn't sure about that, but he tried out a chord, one Shane had taught him. It didn't sound too bad.

"You're a natural!" Oscar declared, though Auden thought he might have been over-exaggerating. "You ever think about being a musician?"

Auden laughed and handed the guitar back. "My musical talents end at paying for concert tickets."

"You never know." Oscar put the guitar back on the wall and straightened it until it was perfect. "Could have a hidden talent."

"I know what my talents are." Auden had known that for many years. "They don't include music."

Oscar shrugged. "Never too late to find out," he said, gesturing at the wall. "After all, not all guitars cost five thousand dollars."

Auden gazed at the Gibsons on display. Maybe Oscar had a point. Gymnastics wasn't everything.

"I hear you have a boyfriend," Anya said, plopping down onto the couch next to Auden. They were down in the lounge area of the dorms, *Survivor 48* playing on television, but mostly Auden was just avoiding going upstairs where he might run into Trayce.

"And where did you hear that?" he asked, though he had a pretty good idea already.

"Just around," she replied, pulling a pillow into her lap. "So is that why you've been acting weird lately?"

"I have not been acting weird," Auden insisted.

"You bought a guitar," she pointed out, ignoring his rolled eyes. "I just assumed the boyfriend was Trayce but apparently you're starting to get out. It's nice. I'm glad you found somebody who might actually care about you."

"Can we not go over this?" he asked, glancing her way, and she shrugged.

"I thought you'd want to talk about it. A new boyfriend. A new lease on life."

"Nothing's changed."

She shook her head. "Yeah, okay. At least tell me his name. How'd you meet him? What do you do?"

"Stop trying to live vicariously through me."

Anya hit him with the pillow. "Shut up. I've got to make sure he's good enough for you. Do I get to meet him? I mean, is he even real? I guess I should have asked that first considering who I heard it from, but..."

"Yes, he's real," Auden replied, rolling his eyes. He knew exactly who she'd heard it from and he wondered what else Trayce had said about Shane. Did it bother Trayce at all that he was seeing someone? He said it didn't, but that didn't necessarily mean it was true.

"Well, do I get to meet him?"

"I don't know." Auden changed the channel, but he wasn't really watching. He wasn't sure he liked the thought of Shane meeting his friends. It would be like crossing two worlds that should never meet.

"You're right," Anya said after a second, and Auden frowned at her. What was he right about? "Trials are practically here. Boy-friends should be the last thing we care about, right?"

"Oh, right," he agreed, changing the channel again. It hadn't been what he'd been thinking.

"And besides, they'll be plenty of time to meet him afterwards, once you're an Olympian. I bet he'll like you even more."

"He's not that shallow."

"I didn't say he was," she insisted, nudging his thigh with her toes. "I'm just saying, an Olympian is much hotter than just some dude with too many muscles."

"So now we've got too many muscles? I thought you had it bad for Liam?"

He could have sworn he saw a faint blush on her cheeks but she shoved his shoulder. "Shut up."

Shaking his head, he changed the channel again.

Auden reached for the next handhold and glanced over at Shane next to him. Shane didn't seem to have as much trouble as Auden did, hauling himself up the fake rock wall with ease. Auden had improved, though, and it wasn't such a fumble to find the next foothold and drag himself upward. He still didn't trust the rope tying him in, but there were instructors below in case anything went wrong.

"Staring at it won't make it any easier," Shane said as Auden paused in climbing.

Auden smiled. "I was just thinking how much better I am than the last time."

"Last time you were terrified of falling on your ass." Shane grinned as Auden pretended to glare. "You do have a very nice ass, though, if it's any consolation."

Shaking his head, Auden laughed and pulled himself up. "I'll take it. So do you."

Climbing up the wall, Auden found that it really was easier, and it was a nice change from gymnastics. He'd thought it would be hard at first, but if he could do a triple salto off the vault, he could climb a wall no problem. Just as long as he didn't fall and break anything.

"So how'd it go?" Shane asked as they reached the top and paused.

"What?"

"The guy," Shane said, watching Auden carefully. "Did you talk to him?"

"I—" Auden hesitated. "I tried. But he's sort of pissed at me."

"Because of me?"

"Well, sort of, but not really I don't think." Auden wasn't sure how to explain what Trayce was mad about. He wasn't even completely sure what it was. "I think he's pissed at me."

"Why? I thought it was just a friends with benefits thing."

"It is—was—I mean, he is my friend and my teammate and I'm just getting so tired of everything to do with gymnastics but I can't escape it. It's everywhere. Everyone's always talking about trials, and they're less a month away now. I don't have much time."

"Are you gonna quit?"

Auden stared at Shane. It wasn't a question anyone had ever asked him, and especially not one he'd ever asked himself. "Quit?" If he'd asked his dad, he would have said that quitting was not an option, especially after all the time and money they had invested in him. Trayce would have probably hit him if he suggested it, and Anya wouldn't believe him. "I can't quit."

"Sure you can," Shane replied, starting back down, and Auden followed slowly. "It's easy. If you're not happy, you just say you're done and be done."

"But I..." Auden didn't know what to say to that. Quitting wasn't allowed and that was that. He couldn't even imagine what would happen if he did quit. Instead of answering, he shut his mouth and followed Shane to the floor where the worker unhooked the safety line.

Shane slid an arm around his waist and smiled at him easily. "You can quit if you hate it so much." He pressed a kiss to Auden's cheek but Auden said nothing. He wasn't sure he liked the unease creeping over him at the suggestion. He chose to ignore it, though, and smiled back at Shane.

"Yeah," he said, heading for the door with Shane and determinedly not thinking about whether Trayce would ever suggest the same.

Auden probably shouldn't have brought it up, but he found himself sitting in the bleachers of the pool with Anya, humidity wafting up from the water, mingled with the sound of shrill whistles from coaches down below. He mainly only came here to admire the long, lean bodies of the swimmers as they did their lengths below.

"You ever think about quitting?" he asked as they watched a swimmer dive off the platform.

"No," she said immediately, frowning at him, though Auden avoided her gaze.

Ever since Shane had brought it up, he couldn't stop thinking about it. Despite the fact that every moment spent in the gym these days felt like torture, he had never once considered simply quitting. Quitting was giving up, was admitting he was afraid of something.

"I'm not quitting until they drag me out kicking and screaming," she went on, tucking back her hair. "Or I win a gold medal. Whichever comes first."

"A lot of people never win gold medals," Auden pointed out, but he knew it was a useless argument.

"A lot of people don't have dreams beyond the normal boring stuff. I'm not going to be one of those people whose only ambition in life is to go to college, get a decent job, and raise a bunch of kids."

"What's wrong with that?" It sounded pretty appealing to Auden — a life of obscurity where there were no expectations, no strings attached to everything he did.

Anya shrugged but she made a face. "It's fine for some people. For some people, that's much better than what they have. But I want more. Don't you?"

"Yeah," he agreed, but gymnastics wasn't all that he wanted. Maybe it had been at one point, but there was so much more out there.

"So why are you talking about quitting?"

"I wasn't. I just asked if you ever thought about it."

Anya shot him a look, turning on the bench towards him. "Why are you thinking about it?"

"I'm not," he tried to assure her, but his chest tightened at her gaze. It was bad enough lying to other people, but lying to Anya felt like something was eating at him on the inside. She'd been one of his best friends since coming to the Center, and even though she couldn't compete, she still stuck around. The only reason Auden could guess was for him.

Anya's eyebrows furrowed, a worried crease on her brow. "Look, you're starting to kind of freak me out," she said seriously. "Why are you talking about quitting? Why have you been late to training? Why have you been blowing Trayce off? What's going on?"

"Nothing is going on," he assured her, looking away, down to the pool. He wondered if swimmers had these kinds of problems. Probably not. Too much water in the brain to think of anything but swimming and getting laid.

"Would you stop lying to me?" Anya demanded, voice growing louder as she turned sharply to face him. "You think I can't tell? You think I believe you when you say nothing is going on? I'm your best friend, Auden. I know you sleep with Trayce but I'm the one who's there for you, so stop lying to me. Tell me what the hell is going on or I swear to God, I will call your dad and tell him you've been wasting his money on concerts and guitars."

"Anya," Auden gritted out, torn between anger and guilt. It wasn't like he told his parents about the concerts—his dad would never support something that wasn't gymnastics, even if it was just for fun.

She didn't budge, though, mouth set in a firm line as she waited. There was no way around it.

Auden sighed and stared down at the pool. One of the swimmers hauled himself out of the water, tiny black shorts clinging to his hips. "I'm just not sure I want to do this anymore."

Anya stared at him for a second. "Do what?"

"This." He gestured around him vaguely. "Training, gymnastics, competitions. It all seems so pointless."

"Pointless?" she repeated, her voice swinging upward at the end in disbelief.

Auden was probably going to regret telling her, but now that he'd gotten started, he couldn't stop himself. It was almost a relief to tell someone who was in the world as well. Talking to Shane was fine, but he didn't really understand. His only solution had been to quit, and as revolutionary as that was, Auden still held back. It was one thing to have Shane suggest he quit—it was another entirely if Anya said the same thing.

"I've been training for years," he said, pushing his hair back in frustration. "Years of my life just so I could, what? Win a gold medal? What is the point?"

"The point is you've been training for too long to give up now!" Anya said, staring at him like she couldn't believe what she was hearing. "Don't you remember why you wanted to do this? It isn't just about gold medals or cereal boxes. Do you think I stick around to torture myself? I can't even do anything for another six months if I'm lucky." She gestured at her shoulder. "That's not why I stay."

Auden shook his head. "There's so much more out there, Anya, beyond the gym and the practices. Don't you ever feel like it's suffocating you?"

"No, I don't," she replied simply, shaking her head at him, worry in her eyes. "Gymnastics is everything I love, and sure, there are other things out there, but nothing so important that I would risk what I have here for it."

"I'm not risking anything—"

"If you want to be a punk rocker or get married and have five kids, that's fine, Auden, but not now! It is not the time for an existential crisis! You have to get your shit together before trials!"

"Can we just stop talking about trials for one fucking minute?" Auden snapped sharply. "Can we just stop it?"

Anya stared at him for a long moment before rising from the bench. "You may not want to talk about it, but they're coming and you're competing in them. Don't freak out on me now."

Auden groaned as she left, dropping his head into his hands. It had been a pipe dream that she might have understood. Everyone at the Center—Anya, Trayce, Dorian—they all had one goal in mind and nothing was going to get in the way of that.

Chapter 12
Practice Doesn't Make Perfect

Auden woke in a slightly unfamiliar room, in a bed bigger than he was used to, Shane curled into a ball on the other side. Sun streamed in through the high, uncurtained window, falling over rock climbing gear piled in a corner. Rolling over, Auden stretched leisurely and smiled to himself. It was a nice change, and he watched Shane sleep for a moment, his eyelids fluttering.

It was strange, waking up next to someone else. He couldn't help thinking of Trayce that night he'd crawled into his bed. He'd woken up the next morning to an empty dorm room and they hadn't spoken of it since. With Shane, Shane asked why he was trying to leave in the middle of the night and pulled him back into bed. A part of Auden felt bad about staying when he still hadn't talked to Trayce about it, but he had stayed anyway.

Finding the time to talk to Trayce wasn't the problem — he saw him enough at training, but finding the actual words seemed impossible. It shouldn't have been so hard to cut it off. Just tell him there was someone else and they were getting serious. That simple, right? Auden grimaced at the thought, at what Trayce might say. If he didn't care, it might hurt even more than Auden expected it to.

Sighing, Auden rolled onto his back and stared at the bright white ceiling. Trials were only two weeks away. Somehow, they'd sneaked up on him, looming over his every waking moment, the constant expectations of everyone around him, the pressure to do well. If he didn't make the team, he didn't even know who would be more disappointed — Dorian, Anya, or his parents.

Shane's phone buzzing startled him out of his reverie and Shane stirred beside him, reaching out and silencing it with a press to the screen. Glancing over, Auden's eyes widened as he realized what time it was.

"Fuck!" he said sharply, tossing back the sheets as Shane rolled over, squinting at him, pillow lines on his face.

"What are you doing?" he mumbled, throwing an arm over his face to block out the light.

"It's nine o'clock," Auden replied, feeling his heart pounding even as he searched for his shirt, but he couldn't remember where he'd left it.

"Yeah, too early," Shane agreed, lifting his arm to watch Auden scour the room for his clothes, but all Auden came up with was his left shoe.

"I'm late for training," he said, panic welling up inside him. Dorian was going to murder him. "Fuck late—I've missed the whole first two hours."

"You start training at seven?" Shane asked, making a face. "Fuck me. Why would you do that?"

Auden didn't answer, digging through a pile of clothes on the floor instead. Why Shane left things on the floor, he didn't know, especially when there was a perfectly good—and empty—laundry basket sitting by his dresser. He was so dead. He couldn't even imagine what Dorian would say. Either he would yell in front of the whole team or else he would fix Auden with a supremely disappointed look. Auden wasn't sure which was worse. Both made his stomach curl into a ball and die.

"Shit, I can't find my clothes!" Auden stood up, throwing the shoe in his hand to the floor.

On the bed, Shane struggled up, still looking sleep rumpled, hair a mess and cheeks pink. "Calm down," he said easily. "You're already two hours late. Why go now? How about you just come back here and we can redo this whole morning wake-up thing."

It was a ludicrous suggestion, completely stupid, but Auden paused. His heart was in his throat at the thought of what Dorian might do to him, but Shane had a point.

Shane shot him a look. "What does training matter anyway? You hate going. At least enjoy your morning."

"Dorian's going to kill me."

"Then he can do it later," Shane said. "Until then, come back to bed."

Shane had a point. Whether he left now or later, he would still have to face Dorian's wrath, and he might as well do it after a nice, relaxing morning. Moving stiffly, Auden crossed the room and slid onto the bed next to Shane.

"Better, huh?" Shane asked, smiling against Auden's mouth as he kissed him.

Auden still didn't feel completely relaxed, a tense buzzing underneath his skin, a feeling of dread building, but he smiled back when Shane pulled away.

"Who needs that stress in your life? Later, we can hit the bar and unwind with some shitty local bands."

"Why don't you play?"

"I've got a gig next week if you want to come."

Auden smiled, letting his fingers trail down Shane's side. "I'd like that."

"It's a date." Shane grinned and pulled Auden in for a slow kiss.

By the time Auden got back to the dorms, it was dark out. It was the first time in years that he had spent a whole day away from the gym. It felt like a guilty pleasure. Walking down the halls, he felt free, completely at ease and not caring a bit that he'd missed an entire day of training. There was no one in the halls as he headed for his room, but as he passed Trayce's door, he heard it creak open behind him.

"Well, you're not dead," Trayce said bluntly, and Auden turned to find him leaned up against the door frame, arms crossed but his shoulders tense.

"Nope, not dead," Auden agreed. He really didn't want to have this conversation with Trayce, not right now when he was in such a good mood.

"Should I even bother asking what the hell you were doing that was so important you missed training?"

Rolling his eyes, Auden turned completely to face Trayce. "You're not my coach."

Trayce barely smiled, tight around the edges. "I'm sure Dorian will have plenty to say tomorrow." He pushed off the frame. "What the hell is going on with you?"

Fine, if Trayce wanted to do it now, they could do it now. Not in the hallway, though. Auden moved past Trayce, careful to keep to himself as he squeezed past him in the doorway. Trayce turned and shut the door slowly behind them, though he didn't make any moves towards Auden as he might have any other day.

Auden glanced around the walls, unchanged as always, filled with gymnastics memorabilia. It looked just like his room.

"I've been meaning to talk to you," he said finally, swallowing down the wave of anxiety that surged up within him. He turned back to Trayce, who stood by the door. "About us."

"Us?" Trayce repeated skeptically.

Auden just had to get this out with as quickly as possible or he would never be able to say it. "You know I've been seeing someone," he said and didn't wait for Trayce to agree. "It's—I think, I think it's getting serious and we have to stop... this."

"This?" Trayce asked, tone sharper this time. He still hadn't moved, but Auden could see the tense line of his shoulders, and as much as he wished it was for the thought of losing him, it probably wasn't.

"You, me," Auden said with a sigh. He hoped Trayce wouldn't make this difficult. "Sleeping together."

Trayce crossed his arms again and was quiet for a moment. Each second that ticked by was agonizing in a way that Auden had never experienced before, not even in competitions.

Finally, Trayce met his eyes, gaze cool. "So you finally found someone," he said. "That's good."

Uneasy, Auden paused. "It is?"

Trayce shrugged, dropping his arms and rounding Auden to the desk. He fiddled with a book and didn't look back at Auden. "It's what you wanted, right?"

"Well..." Auden didn't say that what he wanted was Trayce. "I guess." He watched the back of Trayce's head for a moment.

"Then good for you," Trayce said coldly, turning sharply. He didn't look happy and Auden thought he looked a bit angry. It wasn't Trayce's place to be angry, though. He didn't have any claim over Auden, as he'd said many times. Trayce's anger made Auden angry in return. If Trayce had wanted something more, he could have said so. He didn't have to get mad that Auden had finally found it. "Is that why you've been fucking around for the past few weeks?"

"I missed one training. Big deal," Auden said. As much as he'd like to pretend it wasn't a big deal, he knew better. Still, he didn't need to be told so by Trayce.

Trayce shook his head. "It's one thing to go out and get a boyfriend. It's another to screw over your chances of making the Olympic team. Unless that's what you want to do." He arched a challenging eyebrow at Auden.

"No," Auden said, an automatic response before he could even think about it. "It's none of your business what I do in my free time."

"Fuck whoever you want," Trayce snapped, setting down the book with a sharp thud on the desk. "I don't care, Auden, but you should care about your future."

"Gymnastics?" Auden scoffed. "What kind of a future is that really? Train for fifteen years, compete for ten, and then retire or get injured."

Trayce stilled for a moment, eyes narrowing at Auden. "I'm gonna pretend you didn't say that." He took a step closer to Auden, glancing up and down as though taking his measure and debating violence. "I don't know what your problem is, and I'd suggest a good fuck to get it out of your system but apparently we can't do that anymore."

"No, we can't." Auden stared at Trayce for a moment, searching for a crack in his veneer, but Trayce just looked pissed, not jealous or sad. What did he have to be mad about? His path to the Olympics couldn't be clearer, and what was more, he wanted it. It was more than Auden could say at the moment.

"Then I guess you'll have to go find your boyfriend to do it for you." The way Trayce said boyfriend made it sound like a communicable disease. "Just answer me something — is he everything you

fantasized about?"

"What? I-yes," Auden stuttered, confused at the question, why Trayce was even asking it. What did Trayce care? He said yes before he could even think. Shane wasn't perfect but he was a hell of a lot more than Trayce was to Auden. It was a real relationship, not just fucking and pretending to be friends afterwards. Maybe they hadn't ever really been friends.

Trayce nodded and turned from Auden again, heading to his wall and staring at the posters of old Olympic teams. "Well, that's great," he said bluntly, not sounding happy in the least. "Don't let him fuck up your chances."

"I won't," Auden spat back, anger welling up inside him, both at Trayce's non-reaction and at the insinuation that Shane would get in the way of anything he wanted. He said it before he even thought that he wasn't sure that that wasn't exactly what he wanted.

"Good," Trayce replied shortly. "Now, if you don't mind, some of us plan on attending training tomorrow and need to get to sleep."

Auden stared at Trayce's back, but Trayce didn't turn. It wasn't the worst thing Trayce had ever said to him, but it stung just the same.

"Fine," Auden said, turning with a jerk and leaving. He let the door shut too loudly behind him and glared at it. Fuck. Trayce had barely even reacted except to get angry, angry at what, Auden wasn't sure. He had no right to be. If anyone should have been angry, it should have been Auden. Trayce didn't even care about him enough to be jealous or to try to stop a relationship with Shane. It wasn't his fault that he'd found someone who had actual emotions and was capable of caring about someone else.

He'd asked Trayce enough times why they couldn't be more and every time, Trayce had turned him down flat out. What more was there to say? Auden could be happy with Shane, he told himself as he walked the short way to his dorm. Shane at least didn't have high expectations for his "potential." Shane was content with music and hiking most of the time. Auden didn't have to worry about being anyone but himself around him. He didn't have to pretend to be excited for trials.

In his room, Auden sank onto his bed. The least Trayce could have done was pretend he cared. But he guessed that was too much even for him.

Auden wasn't sure how much longer he could sit in the chair across from Dorian's desk while Dorian lectured him on the importance of not missing training. Half an hour ago, it had been Dorian yelling about irresponsibility and what had Auden been thinking? This close to trials, missing any training was suicide. He was getting sloppy—it was obvious in his routines, Dorian said. Did he have the right kind of drive to be doing this? Was Dorian just wasting his time if Auden wasn't going to take it seriously?

The pit in Auden's stomach had grown so large it felt as though he might just vanish and fall through the floor as Dorian paced in front of him, rubbing his forehead and shaking his head. He glanced at Auden every so often and sighed, seemingly out of words for how disappointed he was.

Auden had come in prepared for this, but he hadn't been prepared for how long it would go on, and how the light feeling from yesterday had vanished and been replaced with resentment. It was just one training. It wasn't as if he'd skipped a week's worth. And his routine was not slipping, he thought grimly. A few mistakes today—he just hadn't stretched enough beforehand. It wasn't anything life-threatening. No one would have believed him if they listened to Dorian go on.

"It isn't just about missing training," Dorian said, finally calm enough that his whole face wasn't red anymore. "I'm starting to question your commitment."

Auden didn't know what to say to that except that he was thinking the same. As Dorian stared him down, he felt shame and annoyance trickling through him.

"Hundreds of gymnasts would kill to have your talent." Dorian squeezed the bridge of his nose as though Auden stressed him out. "If you're scared, that's something we can deal with. I just can't have you missing training. Do you understand?"

Auden nodded. Anything to get out of that room. He could just feel the heaviness of the disappointment in the air and it weighed on him like a ton of bricks.

At long last, Dorian sighed and sank into his chair behind the desk. "That's enough for today," he said, waving at the door. "I don't want to have this talk again, Auden."

Rising, Auden nodded again. "We won't." He left quickly, bumping into Jules in the hallway.

"Auden," Jules said, grinning as usual. "Gonna put on a good show for trials next week, aren't you? I'm looking forward to it."

"Yeah, sure," Auden muttered, hurrying away and hoping Jules could get Dorian to calm down. It certainly wasn't a conversation Auden ever wanted to have again, and he'd have to figure out a way to prevent it.

Chapter 13
Cold Shower

A week wasn't enough time. It wasn't enough time for Auden to figure out what to do. Every day was another day closer to trials, closer to determining his future. A part of him just wanted to quit and give up now. It was what Shane would have suggested. The other part, the one that sounded a bit like both his father and Anya, told him that quitting wasn't an option at this point.

It was with that in mind that Auden went to the bar to see Shane play that night. He didn't want to think about trials or Trayce and the way Trayce had been stubbornly not speaking to him for the past couple days. It made him feel like they were in middle school in the middle of some stupid fight, but not talking to Trayce made Auden both angry and sad at the same time. Why couldn't Trayce just get over himself and be happy for him?

Auden hadn't bothered to tell Anya about their fight considering she would just allude to the fact that they were clearly more than friends and had been the whole time. It wasn't something he wanted to hear again.

At the bar, Auden flashed his fake ID and slipped in amongst the crowd. He didn't see Shane anywhere, and he picked a spot near the side of the stage to wait. When Anya had asked if he was busy tonight, he had told her he'd just be going over old Olympic tapes. He hadn't invited her along. Even if she'd said she wanted to meet Shane, she had also said that boyfriends should be the last thing on their minds right now.

The bar was crowded, and the area near the stage filled up quickly. Auden was surprised considering that aside from Shane, the only other performer was someone he'd never heard of.

It didn't take long for someone from the bar to come up and make the introduction.

"And now, from our very own Tempe, don't throw too many things at Jaeger Blitz!"

The crowd yelled so loud that Auden jumped in surprise. What exactly was he in for? He'd only ever heard Shane play at his apartment, slow and quiet melodies as he tried to teach Auden. The most Auden had picked up so far was the A chord. It turned out he wasn't nearly as talented at the guitar as he was at gymnastics.

A smile grew on Auden's face as Shane came out on stage. Another guy Auden didn't know, one with tattoos covering the entirety of both arms, joined him, taking the place behind the drum kit. Auden hadn't even known Shane was part of a band. He'd just assumed he was a one-man kind of thing, and he was surprised by the guy at the drums nodding at Shane.

Shane didn't bother with greeting the crowd and launched into a fast-paced guitar solo that echoed around the whole room, shaking Auden's bones — angry and passionate and loud all at the same time. It surprised Auden even more that when Shane started singing, the crowd sang along with him.

Give me the end of the world any day.
Give me the drugs to numb the pain.
If it's coming, I'll be ready
So give me the time to find my way and get there fast before we all breathe our last.

Auden watched Shane sing, mouth pressed to the mic, fingers flying over the guitar. Every note was filled with exhilaration and Auden found himself longing for that feeling. It had been so long. It came so easily for Shane here, on stage, surrounded by people shouting his lyrics back at him.

The set went by fast, each song echoed by the crowd. By the end, Shane grinned out at the crowd, catching Auden's eye and shaking his sweaty hair off his forehead.

"You guys rock!" he shouted over the noise. "We'll be back next week for an encore but until then, stay punk!" He stepped back from the mic as it cut off and swung his guitar over his shoulder. Jumping down from the stage, he ignored the people clambering to him and went to Auden. "Good show?" he asked with a grin and out of breath, eyes shining.

"Best I've seen from a shitty local band," Auden agreed, laughing as Shane dragged him closer for a sharp kiss that left him swaying on the spot. "Didn't know you were in a band, though."

"It's just Gavin," Shane said dismissively, glancing over to where the drummer seemed to be enjoying his own crowd of admirers. "Known him forever."

"Well, you were pretty awesome."

Shane grinned. "Glad you think so." He leaned into Auden's ear, lips trailing along it. "I'd so be up for a quickie in the bathroom, but I've got to settle with the owner." He glanced down and Auden held back his groan. Shane wasn't making it easy to ignore the heat pooling in his cock, especially if he wasn't going to do anything about it. Shane smiled. "You'll manage, right?"

Auden had no choice but to nod. He accepted Shane's kiss, wishing he had a few more minutes to spare, but a hot shower would have to do later.

"I'll call you," Shane said, turning to his adoring crowd, and Auden was left with an uncomfortable problem.

Auden turned the water on hot and stepped in the shower. The water almost burned his skin but he let it soak him as he stood under the stream from the shower head. Closing his eyes, he let his hand drift down to his cock and stroke slowly. He'd felt on edge the whole way back from the bar, antsy, and now he would at least get some form of release.

He pictured Shane on stage as he jerked himself off, water glistening on his skin, making the slide easier. He saw Shane's shaggy black hair stuck to his forehead, the shuddering drag of his mouth against the microphone. Gasping, Auden bit his tongue to keep quiet. After all, it was a dorm shower and anyone could walk in.

In his stall, he slid his hand down his cock faster, toes curling against the heat rushing over his skin, a deep flush coupled with the burn of the water. Bracing himself against the tile wall, Auden moved faster. In his mind, he saw Shane grinning at him, but the darkness of the bar faded, replaced with dim, close walls. Shane's hair lightened a shade and became shorter, his face sharper, and Auden came as Trayce swam into his head.

"Fuck," he cursed sharply at the floor as his body tightened, come spilling over his hand. Even as he took a deep breath and straightened up, he didn't feel as though he'd gotten much release.

Washing up quickly, he got out of the shower. He still felt coiled, wound too tightly to do anything, and he didn't know why. Wrapping a towel around his waist, he unlocked the stall and stepped out. The bathroom was brightly lit with shiny tile on the floor and he paused in front of the mirror. His hair stuck to his head and he brushed the water off it.

The door swung open a second later and Auden turned to find himself face to face with Trayce. Trayce paused a second but then stepped around Auden to the sink. He set down the toothpaste in his hand.

Auden sighed. "Are you not talking to me now?"

Trayce glanced at him. "I thought I wasn't allowed to comment on your life anymore."

"Overdramatic much?" Auden asked, annoyed. They were still supposed to be friends. Hadn't that been the whole point of friends with benefits? Why was Trayce the one who was angry? "Aren't we friends?"

Trayce paused and then shrugged. "Sure."

"Okay." Auden frowned at him.

"So, friend, how's the boyfriend?"

It had to be a trap, but Auden answered anyway. "Good. I just went to his show."

"Show?"

"He's in a band."

Trayce nodded and didn't reply, running water over his toothbrush.

Auden watched him, wishing Trayce would just act normally.

They had actually been friends once, before they started this. Now, he was torn between leaving and shoving Trayce up against the sink and kissing him just so things could go back to how they were.

"He goes rock climbing too," Auden went on when Trayce didn't speak. "And hiking and rafting. He does a lot of stuff."

"Well, that's great for him," Trayce muttered, brushing his teeth quickly and spitting into the sink.

"Yeah, it is," Auden replied shortly, annoyed at Trayce and his lack of interest. Trayce must have sensed his annoyance because he straightened up and turned to Auden.

"What do you want me to say, Auden? I'm not dating him."

"You could show a little interest," Auden snapped, hating the way Trayce rolled his eyes. "Instead of being an emotionless asshole."

"You know what's not going to get me a gold medal?" Trayce asked sharply. "Giving a shit about your boyfriend. And it's not going to get you one either."

"You're a dick," Auden said simply, and when Trayce merely shrugged in response, a 'so what?' tilt to his eyebrow, Auden snapped. He pinned Trayce up against the sink in a second, and though Trayce could have escaped, he didn't try, not until Auden's mouth closed over his, the kiss lingering a few seconds too long until Trayce shoved him away.

"I'm not here to make you feel better about yourself," Trayce snapped.

Auden's heart pounded in his chest from the few seconds their lips touched and he ached to do it again, but he didn't. There was Shane to consider. Shane, his boyfriend.

"That's not why I'm talking to you. You're supposed to be my friend, remember?"

"Friend. That's all, remember? Remember when you said it was done?

"So I can't talk to you anymore?"

"If you're gonna keep coming to me, you're not gonna like what I have to say."

"Why do you have to do this?" Auden asked, frustrated. Kissing him had probably been the wrong thing to do but Trayce owed him some sort of explanation.

"And what is that?" Trayce still stood pressed against the sink, hands on the countertop behind him.

"You pretend that what we do doesn't matter—"

"Did. And it doesn't."

"But you get mad when I talk about Shane, when I go out with him."

"Because you're throwing your life away!" Trayce shouted, angrier than Auden had ever seen him. Usually, Trayce was the calm, collected one who didn't let anything ruffle his feathers. Auden was the neurotic one. "You're throwing away your chance to get everything you've ever wanted for some dickbag who cares more about climbing mountains and writing shitty songs just to get in your pants!"

"That is not what's going on," Auden argued. Shane wasn't like that. "And how do you know what I want? How do any of us know what we want? We train all the time—we don't have lives or friends or anything—just so that what? We can get a medal? Do you even remember why you wanted to be a gymnast?"

"Apparently you don't, and that's not my problem." Trayce crossed his arms. "My problem is that you're letting some guy throw you off. You've been shit the past month, ever since you met this guy, and don't tell me that's not why. He's not worth anything in the grand scheme of things. He'll be gone next week when he finds someone with a better ass or whatever he's into."

"You're some guy," Auden shot back. "You're some guy and how much are you worth? You can't even have a real relationship with anyone because of your stupid preconceived notions about love and how it should work. All you know how to do is gymnastics, just like everyone else in this fucking place. That's all they ever think about. Well, there's more out there than the Olympics. It's not a be-all, end-all."

Trayce scoffed, and for a second, Auden thought he might have actually hit a nerve as a flicker of hurt came over Trayce's face. "You're just scared," Trayce said instead. "Scared shitless that you won't make it."

"I am not."

"Yes, you are. You're so fucking scared that you won't make it. I get it. But that doesn't mean I'm gonna let you fuck up your life. We've been training together for three years, Auden, three years of blood, sweat, and tears, all for this one chance, and I'll be damned if you're going to fuck it up."

"Maybe I don't want to be an Olympian!" Auden shouted, and that shut Trayce up. It echoed all around them in the bathroom and an uneasy silence fell in its wake.

Trayce stared at Auden, long enough to make things uncomfortable. Auden didn't know what to say, though. He'd finally said it, and it hadn't made him feel any better. If anything, it made him feel worse from the way Trayce was looking at him, as if he'd never seen him before. At long last, Trayce shook his head.

"That's not true."

"What if it is?"

"It's not," Trayce repeated firmly, glaring at Auden. "You don't even know what you want anymore, but you better figure it out fast because trials are less than a week away, and your routines have been going downhill for a while now. If you don't figure your shit out, you won't make the team."

Auden let Trayce leave and sighed into the silence of the bathroom. Just a few more days and everything would change, for better or worse, although Auden was fairly sure at this point that it would be for worse.

Chapter 14
Pinnacle Peaked

It was Auden's turn next on the floor and he stretched as Liam finished up his routine. He ignored Trayce's gaze from over by the bars. He didn't have anything to say to Trayce right now.

"You're up, Auden," Dorian called, nodding at the mat.

Climbing up, Auden rolled his shoulders and stepped into the corner of the blue mat spreading before him.

"Remember, keep it tight on your tucks and let your center carry you through," Dorian said as Auden prepared himself.

It should have been a routine he could do in his sleep, but Auden found himself stumbling over small steps, a few seconds out of sync with the music. He could feel everything going wrong, feel Dorian's frown even though he couldn't see it. He went out of bounds on the first tumble and took a large step on the second. Everything was just off and he couldn't correct it.

It was just a routine, he told himself firmly as he lined up for the last series of tumbles. He knew it by heart, but his heart wasn't in it as he took off. It was on the landing that he felt the awkward angle of his foot and he went down.

"Shit," he cursed to himself, hitting the mat out of frustration. He took stock of his ankle but it didn't hurt despite the landing.

"Auden." Dorian came over as Auden pushed himself up. "You okay?"

"Fine," Auden replied. "Just missed the landing."

"You need a medic to check it out?"

"It's fine, really, Coach," Auden assured him, walking off the mat and grabbing his water bottle.

"Good," Dorian said, patting him on the back. "Because that might have been the worst routine I've ever seen you do." He sighed. "We leave for trials in a few days, Auden, and let's be honest, you're not up to par as it stands. I want my gymnasts one hundred percent committed to doing their best at the trials. I'm not here to coddle you. I'm here to train you to reach your best potential, and you're not reaching it right now. If you're going to waste your time, then don't waste mine too or your teammates. They want this. They'd gladly take your spot."

Auden glanced at him, uneasy. What was he getting at? He could feel eyes on him, but Dorian thankfully kept his voice down.

"You have to decide if you want this or not," Dorian said seriously. "Because there are other people out there who do, and I don't have time to waste on people who don't. If you're serious, then get serious. If you're not, you know where the door is."

Auden didn't reply as Dorian patted his shoulder and left to watch Liam on the pommel horse. He felt rooted to the spot, unable to move, unable to think or feel anything other than the gaping hole inside him. He caught Trayce's gaze from across the room and that was what snapped him out of it. Dorian was right. If he didn't want to be there, he didn't have to be.

Digging in his bag, he pulled out his phone and dialed Shane's number.

"Hey," Shane greeted him easily.

"Hey."

"Uh oh. You sound stressed."

"I just want to get out of here," Auden said, glancing around the gym. Being here was so suffocating, under Dorian and Trayce's gazes.

"Want to go to the Wall?"

Auden hesitated. "How about we go climbing outside?"

Shane paused and then Auden heard the smile in his voice. "You want to climb outside? What about the scorpions?"

"I'm ready."

"Okay," Shane agreed. "I'll pick you up in an hour, how about that?"

"Sounds perfect." Auden just had to get out of there. He hung up and grabbed his bag. He was done training for the day.

Luckily for Auden, the sky was somewhat overcast, a grey haze covering the sun as they stood at the foot of the mountain. Auden wouldn't have even known it was there if Shane hadn't taken him there. Shane handed him the gear and helped him clip on the ropes.

"You sure you're not afraid of the bugs?" Shane asked as he rubbed on sunscreen. Auden shook his head, glancing up at the vertical rock wall. It was more like a cliff than anything else with barely any places to step or pull himself up.

He just wanted to forget about everything Dorian had said, everything that Trayce had said. He just wanted to forget about everything. If he had to touch a few insects to do it, then so be it.

Shane tightened the safety rope to his belt and smiled at Auden. "Let's do it."

It was harder than in the climbing gym, and Auden felt about ten times more precarious out here. Shane stood below, threading the rope through the belay, waiting for Auden to pull himself up.

"So what happened?" Shane asked as Auden climbed, moving slowly along the rock cliff.

Searching for a grip, Auden sighed. "I don't know. Trials are days away and my routines are getting worse, and I just don't know what to do."

"I told you, you should just quit," Shane said, tightening the rope.

The rock crumbled under Auden's feet. "It's not that simple." He grabbed another piece of rock. "I've been doing this for fifteen years."

"Time means nothing. Don't waste your time doing something you don't like."

"I don't not like it, I just..." Auden didn't know where to go with that. "It's complicated. Everything was fine until World Championships. After that, it just sort of fell apart." He moved upward, careful to find sturdy handholds and footholds, although it was difficult on what seemed to be easily crumbled rock.

"I say you're better off," Shane said from below him. "Who needs that shit? Besides, competitive sports are such a waste of time."

Auden frowned, glancing down as he reached up. "What does that mean?"

"They're just a way for society to project physical prowess as a good trait and overpay athletes to do something that doesn't help anyone. What's the point? Society spends millions, billions, of dollars on athletes who contribute nothing but mindless entertainment for the under-educated."

Auden stared down at Shane, unable to believe what he was hearing. Shane couldn't be serious. He opened his mouth to say so as his hand landed on a rock, but a second later, something very large and hairy brushed against his fingers and he jerked back.

In that moment, he lost his grip. Reeling back, he felt himself falling, the rope barely tightening as he felt gravity pulling him down, the ground rushing up to meet him.

"Auden!" Shane called sharply.

Auden shut his eyes as he fell, hands fumbling for the rope at his belt. There was too much slack below, not enough tension on the belay. Seconds before he hit the ground, he was pulled up sharply, Shane grabbing the rope. The rope slowed his fall, but it wasn't enough to stop the whole impact as he hit.

He couldn't breathe. For a moment, everything rushed around him, his diaphragm seizing up from the impact as he lay there, staring at the grey sky. Fuck, he couldn't breathe. As he lay there, gasping for air, he saw his whole life disappearing, vanishing before his eyes.

He was ten years old, begging his parents to let him train with a professional coach, writing a five page report on why it was a good idea to let him pursue gymnastics beyond the kiddie classes. His dad said it was merely a passing obsession.

He was sixteen, handing his dad a fiscal report he'd spent a week preparing, researching costs on the internet, and praying it would be enough to let him move away to train at the Center, to train under Dorian Stuart, the former Olympian. His dad inspected the report and spent two more days scribbling calculations before agreeing to it.

He was eighteen, winning his first gold at Worlds, and Trayce smiled at him as he came off the podium, pulling him into a hug and saying, "When the Olympics come around, we're gonna own that shit. You and me, Auden."

Auden gasped for breath, flat on his back as he stared at the hazy Arizona sky, rocks and dirt digging into his back. No more gymnastics, no more competition, no Olympics or trials. Everything he'd ever worked for gone in one stupid fall, one stupid mistake.

The pressure on his chest didn't ease even as air flooded his lungs. One fall and he could have ruined everything. He'd worked so long for the Olympics and here he was tossing it away for what? For a guy? For a desperation to feel something other than fear? What had he been thinking?

"Auden?" Shane hurried over, unclipping his rope and leaning over him. "You okay? Can you get up?"

Sucking in air as it returned to his lungs, Auden barely nodded. "I just, I just knocked the wind out of me, I think." He felt a little dizzy as he sat up, taking deep breaths. He'd never quite appreciated breathing as much as he did right then.

"You're fine," Shane assured him. "The rope caught you. It was just a little fall."

"A little?" Auden repeated, taking the water bottle Shane offered. "I could have died."

"Not died. It was barely six feet." Shane didn't sound very concerned which miffed Auden. Falling six feet onto hard ground could have done some serious damage. He'd fallen enough to know it.

"Seriously injured then, and that would have completely ruined my whole career."

Shane shook his head as he helped Auden up. "What career? You don't even like it."

"I do," Auden argued. "I just fell off a mountain and all I could think was that I could never do gymnastics again."

"Wouldn't that be a good thing?"

"It would be the worst thing!" Auden brushed the dirt off his jeans and turned to Shane. He paused, Shane's words coming back to him, the reason he'd been distracted in the first place. "Did you say that competitive sports were a waste of time?"

Shane shrugged. "They are. I don't know why you care so much. Besides, you have to have fallen a thousand times before."

"In a gym with medics all around, in a controlled environment. This is completely different. What if I'd broken my ankle? What if I had to get stitches?"

"It's just gymnastics."

"It isn't to me."

"It was until two minutes ago," Shane replied, frowning at him. "Ever since I met you, it was all, 'I hate gymnastics.' And now you've changed your mind."

"I never said I hated it."

"You didn't have to."

"I was scared, okay?" Auden snapped. "I'm terrified I won't be good enough for trials. As soon as I won at Worlds, everyone just started assuming I'd make the team, and what if I don't? I've wanted this for so long. I don't even know what I would do if I didn't make it."

"Who cares?" Shane asked loudly, talking over him. "It's just some stupid competition, some pissing contest for countries to pretend they're better than each other."

"Competitive sports teach good sportsmanship, teamwork, and give you a goal to work towards."

Shane began rolling up the rope. "You sound like an Afterschool Special."

"So you think what I do is pointless?" Auden stared at him as Shane shrugged.

"Pretty much. There are better things to do. It's a huge waste of time."

"You think I wasted fifteen years of my life?"

"Yeah."

Auden couldn't believe it. Even if Shane had always been disinterested in gymnastics, he hadn't expected this. Everything seemed to hit him at once, like a rock to the head—something he'd almost had a few minutes ago. He had been scared, just like Trayce had said. There was so much pressure to do well, so much pressure to not let anyone down, to make it to the Olympics like he'd dreamed about for so many years. He hadn't started gymnastics because he wanted to win a medal—he'd done it because he loved the sport. Sure, there were other things out there but there was nothing like gymnastics, not for him.

He'd wasted so much time, he realized as he stood there watching Shane pack up the equipment. The last two months had been entirely wasted, doing everything in his power to avoid the thought of trials. Fuck, he was so far behind in his training. He'd let everything slip and it was entirely his fault.

Glancing at Shane, he paused. "I think you're right. I have been wasting time."

"That's what I said," Shane said. "Athletes are just overpaid, over-appreciated people who are no better than the rest of us, and you'd be better off quitting and getting a real hobby."

"Hobby?" Auden repeated. He could just imagine how angry Trayce would have been if he'd heard Shane call it that. He shook himself, though. That wasn't the point. "I meant with you. I didn't know that was how you felt about sports, and I don't think we should keep dating."

Shane paused as he stuffed the rope in his bag. "You're breaking up with me because I think competitive sports are stupid?"

"I'm breaking up with you because Olympic trials are in three days and I should be around people who believe I can make it, not people who think my whole life has been a waste of time."

Shane stared and then shoved the rope in the bag. "You're lucky we even went out," he said. "All professional athletes are self-centered assholes. I thought maybe you'd be different."

Auden glared at Shane. "I thought musicians were supposed to be open-minded, but I guess I was wrong."

"Whatever," Shane sneered. "I hope you enjoy your Olympics and your worthless piece of metal."

Stalking past him, Auden didn't reply. He had bigger things to worry about than Shane, like getting his routines back on track in just three days before his whole gymnastics career went up in smoke.

Chapter 15
Out of Time

The swing should have been easy, a lift with the arms, twisting on the rings, but Auden felt the rings shake under his grip, and when he released half a second too early, he couldn't carry through the landing. It was too late to stop it, and he landed on his knees, hands hitting the mat. At least it hadn't been his head.

Dorian stood with his arms crossed on the edge of the mat but he let Auden push himself up. Dusting off his hands, Auden sighed. The rings weren't even the most difficult event and he couldn't even land that. There was just too much to think about, and he knew he shouldn't be thinking about anything at all that could distract from the routine.

He didn't have much time left, though. They left for trials in just a few days, and so far, he'd messed up all his routines, as though his body couldn't remember how they went. He felt strangely rusty as though the past month had taken everything he knew about gymnastics and thrown it out the window. He couldn't stop thinking about Shane and what he'd said. Auden had wasted so much time for something that had meant nothing. He'd almost lost everything, and he still would if he couldn't get his act together soon.

Dorian nodded Auden over. Dread — the dread that seemed permanently lodged in his stomach — rose in Auden as he joined Dorian at the edge of the mat.

Sometimes, Auden wondered what Dorian would be like if he wasn't his coach, but something told him that Dorian was this serious about everything in his life.

"Auden," Dorian said, not sounding angry or annoyed but simply calm, "I think it's time we made a decision."

"Decision?" Auden asked, unsure. Behind him, Trayce was working on his floor routine, and Auden turned away from him. They hadn't talked since that fight in the bathroom, and Auden wasn't even sure what he was supposed to say, what he wanted to say.

"We leave for trials in two days," Dorian said bluntly. "It's the chance of a lifetime for any gymnast, but you have to decide if it's really what you want."

"It is," Auden said swiftly, cutting off whatever else Dorian might have said. He may have wasted the past couple months but now more than ever, he knew what he wanted. He had let the pressure get to him, had let everyone else's expectations of him cloud his judgment, but that was over. The only thing he wanted now was to make the Olympic team and prove everyone right.

Dorian eyed him for a long moment, as though assessing his answer. Auden felt as though he were under a microscope with Dorian staring at him. He'd fucked up. He knew that. It wasn't something he was proud of and he couldn't say he'd seen it coming.

Finally, Dorian dropped his arms and rubbed his forehead. "If you're sure. I don't want anyone there who doesn't want to be there. Everyone else in this room has been dreaming of their chance and it's not fair to them or to yourself if you aren't."

Auden shook his head, swallowing down the fluttering nerves in his throat. "I do. I swear." He didn't tell Dorian about his doubts, the occasional surety that he wasn't good enough, that even if he did manage to fix his routines, he still wouldn't make it and how crushing that would be.

"Alright. Let's run it again." Dorian patted his back once and nodded at the rings.

As Auden stepped onto the mat, he glanced over and caught Trayce watching him. Trayce looked away the second their eyes met, though, and the tangled mess in Auden's stomach tightened worryingly instead.

An owl hooted outside the dorm window, but otherwise, the night was quiet—no footsteps in the hall, no snatches of hushed conversation. Everyone was in bed and probably asleep, everyone except Auden, who lay on his bed, eyes on the dark ceiling. A bright yellow light snuck in through the gaps in the curtains, gilding a long sliver of the ceiling in light.

He should have been asleep, preparing for another long day of training that would inevitably end much the same as today, with disappointment and shame. The routine wasn't the problem—he was. He'd let himself get dragged away, let himself think it wasn't important anymore. Groaning, Auden rolled over and pressed his face to the pillow.

He was glad it was dark and he couldn't see the photos lining the walls. Past Olympic winners would do nothing to bolster his confidence at a time like this. They were just a reminder of what he'd almost given up. Opening his eyes against the pillow, he sighed. There had to be something he could do.

As he lay there, Shane's face appeared in his mind. Just thinking about Shane made him feel queasy. How could he have spent so much time with someone and known so little? He hadn't even bothered to ask or go much beyond the physical. Maybe that was his problem.

He rolled onto his back. His hands twitched, restless, unable to sit still though he knew he should sleep. His routine wasn't likely to get better if he stayed up all night worrying. He thought of Trayce, just a few feet down the hall, probably asleep with his mouth open, one hand tucked under the pillow. Trayce didn't have these problems—he wouldn't because Trayce didn't let other people get in the way of what he wanted.

The owl hooted again, somewhere in the distance, this time echoed by the cries of coyotes, but they wouldn't be anywhere nearby. Frustrated, Auden rubbed his face vigorously. He needed to sleep, but he couldn't. He kept replaying the day's training over and over in his head. There had to be something he could do. Something.

Giving up would have been so easy, he thought as he lay there, listening to the silence of the dorm around him. It wasn't the answer he wanted. He had to turn it around somehow.

Kicking off the sheets, Auden sat up, pushing back his hair and gazing into the darkness. If he wasn't going to sleep, he could at least do something. He pulled on a pair of sweatpants and a tee-shirt in the darkness, not even sure where he would go. Nothing was open on campus at this time of night, and he didn't have a car to go into town. He just couldn't stay in the dorm one more minute, not with his future hanging in the balance.

There was one place he could go, he thought, standing in the middle of the room, a shoe in one hand. One place that was always open if you knew your way around. The backdoor of the gym was always unlocked, forgotten by the absent-minded janitor. It was Auden's only hope, and he grabbed his key off the table without a second thought, leaving the dorm and the silence.

Auden wasn't supposed to be in the gym alone, and the equipment looked desolate before him. He wasn't sure it was possible for a blue floor mat to mock him, but it sure felt that way. For a long moment, he stared out across the gym.

The first time he'd come to EGC, the gym had seemed huge, looming over him, brimming with possibilities, with hope for an Olympic future. When had he lost that? Had he ever lost it? Maybe it had just gotten jumbled up with fear.

He only had this chance to make up for his mistakes the past few months and prove to himself and to everyone else that he wanted it.

How was he supposed to do that, though? It felt as though his routines were slipping away from him, going through the motions with nothing much special about them. He'd used to relish learning new tricks, but these days, the most important thing was being con-sistent.

Consistency bred boredom.

Stepping up to the high bar, Auden paused. His routine, as it stood, was solid, boring, and he felt it every time he did one. Even if he did manage to do them correctly, something was dragging him down. He'd tried not to think of Shane since that day on the moun-tain, but his words came floating back as he gazed up at the bar.

"Can't be afraid to take a chance."

Auden had taken a chance—he'd taken a chance on Shane and where had it gotten him? Distracted and rapidly losing whatever chance he had at making the Olympic team. He had to turn his routines around, but aside from constant practice, he couldn't think of what to do.

As much as Auden had already taken chances—the wrong chances lately—there was one left. Dorian had mentioned it months ago, but he hadn't taken it to heart. It had seemed like a ploy, a simple attempt to gain more points in a routine, but maybe there was something more. Difficulty levels could make or break a routine, and what did he have to lose at this point?

Moving over to the training mat, Auden paused at the start. At the end, large foam mats sat to catch him if he didn't make the landing. Most of his layouts were good, made to fit his abilities, a few to up the difficulty level, but he'd been training for years now. If he wanted to make the team, he had to take a chance.

It was something he'd only tried a few times and it had never gone particularly well—Dorian had said that it was better to do a skill you knew you could complete than to break your neck attempting something else. His heart battered in his chest just at the thought of attempting a triple twisting double back again. The last time, he'd fallen on his ass and Dorian had suggested a double pike instead.

A double pike wasn't good enough.

Auden thought about the form; in theory, a triple twisting double back was a simple move, but nothing was simple when it came to layouts. Dorian would murder him if he attempted this and it ended badly. He was already breaking the rules by training alone. In the back of his mind, he knew it was stupid but he was running out of time, and the only way he was going to make the team was if he took a chance. He had to go all out this time, forget about Shane and Trayce and his worries about trials. He just had to do it.

Swallowing down the nerves crawling in his stomach, he faced the long runway and drew in a breath. Before he could question his sanity, he took off, building up speed until he hit the middle of the mat, going into a back flip then another. As he pushed off the mat, he squeezed his body together, trying to keep control as he whipped through the air, one twist and then two, and then a third, but he was already too close to the ground to open up and hit the mat on his hands and knees.

For a second, it felt as though he couldn't breathe, not out of injury but just mere fear that gripped him as his knees hit the mat. If it had been the real mat, not the foam pads, it would have been worse.

Leverage, he thought, forcing air through his lungs and pushing himself up. He needed more leverage to get the third twist. He returned to the start of the mat and gave himself a shake. Gymnastics wasn't about fear. You couldn't be afraid to do stunts—that was what separated the casual gymnasts from the hardcore trainers. If he'd been afraid of falling, he never would have made it this far.

His second attempt flew by in a blur—a good double back, but he felt it coming before it happened, the sharp twist in his gut as he came out of the third twist and landed, legs barely beneath him, not enough height to catch him as he slammed to the foam mats, skidding on his ass. Frustrated, he sat there for a moment. It would have been so easy to just give up and tell Dorian that he couldn't do it—that he couldn't go to trials. Just like Shane had said, he could just quit, but that wasn't what he wanted. It had never been what he wanted. He'd just wanted someone to tell him it was okay to be selfish, to feed his own fears about his future, to run away from his problems.

He'd been completely stupid, but he wasn't going to let it happen again. Standing up, he brushed himself off and headed for the start of the mat. He would master this and any other skills he needed to make that team, no matter what it took.

"Ugh, I'm so jealous." Anya pouted as she sat on the end of Auden's bed while he debated throwing in yet another pair of socks to his suitcase.

"Jealous that I'm about to ruin my only chance at being an Olympian?" He tossed the socks in anyway. He didn't mention his late-night practices or how many times he'd fallen on his ass trying to get the triple twist just right. There was still a lot of work to do but at least Dorian hadn't frowned so much today in practice.

Anya rolled her eyes and grabbed a copy of *Gymnastics Monthly* off his desk. "You are not going to fail. You're going to be fine."

"Have you not been paying attention?" Auden asked. "My routines are crap. I can't stick a landing to save my life. Trayce isn't even speaking to me, and trials are in three days."

Anya flipped a page. "This is the part in all the sports' movies where the team rallies and comes off with a victory anyway."

"This isn't a movie. It's real life." Huffing, Auden sunk onto the bed. He was only halfway packed, but it felt like he was packing for his doom. There was so much to do, and as much as he wanted to believe that he wasn't creating a recipe for disaster by training alone, he wasn't so sure. "Besides, who are you supposed to be in this movie?"

"I'm the plucky best friend, under-appreciated for her greatness, who gives you the courage to get on that plane and make your Olympic dreams come true."

"Shouldn't you be giving some sickly sweet speech about perseverance and beating the odds right about now?"

"Like you said, this isn't a movie." She set down the magazine and turned towards him. "And you don't need a speech. You're the best gymnast here, aside from me, of course." She grinned. "And I know you're going to be fine."

Auden wished he had her confidence. Every time he missed a landing, it was harder to get up. "It's easy for you to say—you don't have to worry about competing."

"You think I wouldn't be terrified right now if I had trials in a few days? I would be panicking. I mean, sure, I am a great gymnast, but it's scary. Competitions are always scary, but you know, Auden, it's just like every other time. You've won before and you'll win again."

Auden smiled. "You don't call that a speech?"

Anya shoved his shoulder playfully. "You don't need me to tell you you're great. You don't need anyone."

Auden gazed at his half-filled suitcase. In a couple days, he'd be in Raleigh, North Carolina, all the way across the country. Anya wouldn't be with him. It'd be just him, him and the rest of his teammates. Trayce. Trayce would be there.

"What? What's wrong?" Anya asked when he didn't speak for a moment.

Auden sighed, wondering if he should even say it. "I just wish I hadn't met Shane. He screwed everything up."

"I hate to be the bearer of bad news, but Shane didn't screw anything up. You made a mistake trusting him. It was stupid, yes, but everybody does it."

"So it's my fault?"

"Honestly? Yeah," Anya said, but she patted his arm when he frowned. "But it's okay 'cause you're gonna fix it."

"I don't think I can fix everything."

"Trayce?"

Auden shrugged. There wasn't much to say on the subject. "He won't even talk to me."

"Have you tried talking to him?"

"No," he admitted, but what was he supposed to do? Trayce still didn't want the same things as him. Even if he admitted that Trayce been right, it wouldn't solve anything. Auden had been completely wrong about Shane and thinking about it made him feel angry. Shane had been against everything that Auden was—his whole life's pursuit—and he hadn't even known it. He hadn't even cared to ask. He'd just used Shane as an escape from his problems and he deserved what he got for that.

He doubted Trayce would see it that way, though.

"Why's he mad at you, anyway?" Anya asked, refolding the shirts in Auden's suitcase.

"We had a fight about Shane and training. I don't know." He didn't really know what it meant. Trayce was just frustrated with him, he guessed. He almost couldn't blame him considering how he'd been acting the past few weeks.

Anya hummed thoughtfully and placed the shirt back. "Maybe he was jealous."

"Trayce doesn't get jealous," Auden said simply. "He's just mad 'cause I've sucked the past few weeks in training."

Anya shot him a look. "I know you're teammates and semi-friends sometimes, but people don't get that mad because you missed a practice or didn't stick your landing. They only get that mad because they care."

"Well, we are friends."

"Auden." Anya sighed as though put-upon. "How many times do I have to say this? You're more than friends."

"Fine. We are, sometimes, but he doesn't see it that way so I shouldn't either." It hurt to admit it, even though he'd always known. Like everyone always said, someone always gets hurt in relationships like these. This time, it was Auden. At this point, though, Trayce should have been the least of his worries.

"Look, don't worry about Trayce," Anya said, patting his knee gently. "It'll work itself out. Things always do. Just worry about sticking your landings and getting back to how you were at World's. If you can do that, you can make the team."

"Thanks for the vote of confidence." Auden shook his head but smiled when Anya did.

"That's what the plucky best friend is for. Although, four years from now, you'll have to be my plucky best friend when I go to trials."

"You know I will be," Auden assured her. "Though you probably won't have the same problems."

Anya shrugged. "I'm sure I'll have something for you to fix."

Auden laughed and rose from the bed. He had to finish packing, after all.

Chapter 16
Taking Chances

Though the hour had grown late, the sun had yet to sink behind the mountain, instead hanging low and casting a golden glow over the campus, gilding the fading yellow flowers of the Palo Verde tree in dusk. Few people were out, but Auden still felt completely obvious as he left the dorm and headed for the gym. It was hard enough to sneak out at night, but in broad daylight, it was even more conspicuous. Tonight was his last chance to get in some more practice before they left for trials tomorrow.

Shouldering his bag, he glanced around, making sure the coast was clear. If he was caught, he would be in big trouble from the coaches, and he might be pulled from competing in the trials before he even had the chance. It was a risk he was willing to take, though.

Down the winding path, he pretended he was heading for the cafeteria, though it was closed by now.

"Auden!"

He wasn't twenty feet from the dorm when a voice brought him to an abrupt stop. He'd been caught.

"Auden," came the voice again, and he recognized it.

Turning sharply, he frowned at Shane crossing the grounds, not bothering to use the path, darting around a barrel cactus. A mixture of emotions rose in Auden as he stood there — annoyance, unease, confusion.

"What are you doing here?" he asked as Shane reached him. He thought he'd made it pretty clear that they'd broken up.

Shane hitched on a half-smile and shoved his hair back, sweat glistening on his forehead. "It's been a couple days and I hadn't heard from you."

"Because we broke up," Auden replied, shifting back on his heels, shoulders straightening.

"Well, if you're going to run away every time we disagree," Shane said with a grin, "then we have a lot of work to do."

"Disagree?" Auden repeated and his bag dropped to the ground. "You think that the thing I've dedicated my life to is pointless."

"No need to take it so hard," Shane said, shaking his head as though Auden just didn't get it. "It's just a sport. It's a hobby, like rock climbing. You're so overdramatic, but that's okay, Auden."

Auden couldn't believe him, trying to pass it off as not important. Instead of arguing, he crossed his arms and fixed Shane with a glare.

"What are you doing here?"

"I was trying to talk to you. You're making it kind of hard. Look, Auden, if this relationship is gonna work, we have to talk about stuff."

"I—" Auden didn't even know what to say. Every word that came out of Shane's mouth just made him angrier, both at Shane and at himself. How could he have let himself throw everything away for someone who thought that a pitiful apology would make things okay? "You have no idea why I'm mad, do you?"

"You're upset I don't care about gymnastics, but lots of people disagree about sports. My parents like two completely different football teams but they make it work."

"This is not remotely the same as liking two different sport's teams," Auden pointed out bluntly. Glancing around, he felt exposed standing in the middle of the pathway, his bag on the ground next to him. Behind him, he heard the door to the dorms swing open but he didn't look to see who it was. No one walked past, though.

Shane seemed to bristle, as though Auden just wasn't listening. He reached for Auden's hand, but Auden pulled it out of the way. He frowned. "The point is, you're throwing in the towel too soon! I fucking like you, Auden, and you can't just walk out when we fight. You got to give me a chance to apologize."

"Is that what this is supposed to be? 'Cause I haven't heard an apology in all that."

Shane took a step forward, his smile faltering to reveal a mixture of exasperation and annoyance.

"Fine. I'm sorry you took what I said so hard, but the thing is, I really do like you, Auden. In fact, I think I might even love you." Auden stared as the words came out of Shane's mouth. They hit him like a freight train run off the rails, smacking into him and knocking any response he might have had out of his brain. It was insane. Shane was insane. Behind him, the dorm door swung open and shut again. He glanced back but all he saw was a dark head vanishing inside.

"That's impossible," he said at length, gathering together his wits and trying to ignore the desperate look in Shane's eyes. "We barely know each other."

"I know you're obsessive about gymnastics and being perfect. I know you take sugar in your tea even though you're not supposed to. I know—"

"But you don't *know* me," Auden interrupted sharply, taking a step back from Shane. "Those are just facts, things everyone knows."

"I think I know what I feel," Shane replied, sounding annoyed. He shoved a hand through his hair again, too rough, frustration leaking through his movements. "I love you."

"Stop saying that." Auden grabbed his bag and started down the path again, hoping Shane wouldn't follow, but he wasn't that lucky.

"I won't," Shane said, catching up to him and matching his quick pace. "You called me, you know, and asked me out. You wanted to try something different and I took you climbing. Without me you'd still be hitting the gym with no hope of winning whatever it is."

Auden stopped sharply to glare at Shane, annoyance bubbling deep within him. The simple fact that Shane didn't care at all about gymnastics would have been enough, but to say he had no hope was a blow he couldn't stomach. Whatever Shane thought—that he was in love with him—Auden certainly wasn't in love with Shane, and he wasn't going to let Shane jeopardize his chances at an Olympic run.

"I'm leaving for trials tomorrow," he said, forcing himself to stay calm and not hit Shane. "I don't have time for this. So just leave me alone."

"We'll talk when you get back then," Shane said and Auden sighed.

"No. It's over. This is it. I'm done. I don't care if you think you love me. I don't love you."

"It's because of that guy, isn't it?" Shane snapped, his expression darkening, any hints of sympathy leaving his face. "That other guy you were seeing?"

Auden shook his head, frustration building inside him. "This has nothing to do with Trayce. There is only one thing that I really love right now, and it's gymnastics. So just go home, Shane."

"Fuck you," Shane spat, grabbing Auden's arm as he started to turn. "If it wasn't for me, you'd still hate your life. I'm the only one that cares about you. This Trayce guy doesn't even give a shit about you."

Wrenching his arm out of Shane's grip, Auden shoved him back, away from him. "I'm not gonna thank you for nearly getting me killed. But you're right about one thing; you made me realize how stupid I was to ever consider giving this up. I almost did, and for what?" He eyed Shane, Shane's once handsome face contorted in anger. How could he have even considered giving up something he'd worked so hard for, just so someone like Shane could like him?

Shane's lip curled as he straightened up, a haughty look in his eye. "All you gymnasts are fucked up. But fine. Fuck you, Auden! When you lose, don't come crying to me!"

Auden turned on his heel then and strode away, not even caring if anyone saw him head for the gym. He just had to get away from Shane. It was too much. He couldn't deal with the stress of competition along with Shane showing up and declaring his misguided love for him. At least he'd seen his true colors before he'd actually fallen too far. They barely knew each other, and sex didn't count as love.

Auden slipped in the gym doors and held them shut, glad when Shane didn't follow or pound on the doors. He didn't need that kind of drama. It was over. What he needed right now was to focus and nail his skills. He needed to pray it would be enough.

Sitting in the waiting area at Sky Harbor, Auden shifted in the uncomfortable chair. Outside the large windows, airplanes rolled past. He was barely awake, but Dorian had shuffled them onto a bus an hour ago and they'd been waiting at the airport ever since. The sun crested over the horizon, painting the sky a pale yellow and blue, orange and pink creeping up behind. Palm trees waved in the early morning breeze in the distance.

Pulling out his phone, he brought up a video. His thumb hovered over the play button, unsure he wanted to rewatch it. It was his World Championship routine, something that had been so perfect at the time. It felt now like it had been a completely different person six months ago at that competition. He'd been so confident, sure in his ability to win medals and get his routines right. Now, he wondered if he was making a mistake even going to trials. Wouldn't it have been better to skip it and try again in four years? He didn't want to wait that long. This was his chance now and he had to take advantage of it, no matter what had happened lately.

A sudden movement across from him distracted him from playing the video. Looking up, he found Trayce sprawled in the chair, leg propped up, his bag dumped on the floor. He said nothing to Auden, scrubbing a hand through his hair and glancing around the airport.

This was Auden's chance to say something, to apologize or explain or something. The words didn't come, though. After a minute, Trayce's eyes flicked to him. His gaze was guarded, a cold stiffness to his shoulders despite being draped over two seats.

"Surprised to see you here," he said at long last. "I thought you didn't want to be an Olympian."

Auden felt the chill in Trayce's words. "I didn't know what I wanted." It wasn't an apology, and he almost grimaced as soon as he said the words. He didn't, though, watching Trayce's eyes narrow, the way he looked away, shaking his head.

Cursing himself, Auden cast around for something else to say, something to smooth over the choppy waves crashing in his stomach, making him feel queasy. It wasn't even about the trials; it was about Trayce. Somehow, he'd let him down even if he'd never known whether Trayce had any expectations of him. He'd thought Trayce's whole point had been that what they had meant not having expectations.

"That's obvious," Trayce muttered. "But I suppose you want the musician now. Is he coming along later?"

Auden didn't get the chance to reply as Liam showed up, shoving Trayce's leg off the seat and plopping down next to him. Instead, he settled for frowning at Trayce. Since when did Trayce have the right to be mad at him for dating Shane?

"Granola bar?" Liam offered, unwrapping his own.

Auden shook his head and Trayce ignored him completely, digging out his phone and putting in his earphones. It was going to be a long flight.

The facilities were much as Auden had expected with the same equipment as they had in Phoenix. As they entered, he saw a few people he recognized from meets, but he didn't acknowledge them, nor them him. Beside him, Dorian seemed satisfied, taking in the gym.

"Alright," he said, turning to the team. "Go get changed then we'll do some warm-ups and a few quick run-throughs. There isn't much time today, and tomorrow, trials begin. I don't want you to be nervous. I don't want you to be afraid. I want you to be confident. You're all talented and I'm proud whether or not you make the team. Now get going."

Auden headed for the locker room with the rest of the team, but despite Dorian's words, he couldn't help but feel worried. His routines hadn't improved and there was no time left. He had really screwed himself over all because he couldn't admit that he was afraid.

In the locker room, he changed into his workout gear, listening to the excited conversations of the other guys.

"Any word who the judges are?"

"Dunno yet. Just hope they don't have a stick up their ass like four years ago."

"Any bets on who'll make it?"

Auden stared at his locker as he listened. He didn't even know the guys talking, but somehow it still felt like they were talking about him.

"You don't know until you know," the other said, shutting the locker with a slam. They left the room, and Auden sighed.

Glancing over, he found Trayce pulling on his shirt, head bowed towards the floor. All he wanted to do was kiss him and admit he'd been wrong about Shane, but that wouldn't have solved anything, so he shut his locker and left for the gym instead.

Out on the floor, Dorian put Auden to work stretching out his muscles. Auden tried to ignore the other gymnasts around him, ignore their chatter, their bets on who would make the team. After all, there were only five spots open and just a few alternate spots. Considering how many gymnasts there were, the odds weren't good even for the ones who hadn't been messing up all their routines lately.

"Auden," Dorian called. "Let's run through your high bar."

Nodding, Auden pushed himself off the mat, stretching out his shoulders. He had to be loose, flexible, not tight and worrying about things he couldn't control.

The assistant coach lifted him up to the bar and Auden took a second to focus. He needed to focus. He needed to let go of everything that had happened, let go of Shane's voice in the back of his head telling him that competitive sports were a waste of time and money, get rid of his dad's voice ranting about how much the Center cost him every year and how he better make it worthwhile. He had to remember why he wanted to be a gymnast, why he'd spent the last fifteen years of his life working towards this singular moment.

His bars routine wasn't the most difficult, and he kept it low-key. He didn't want to let on to Dorian that he'd been practicing on his own, not yet. If Dorian knew, he would be in huge trouble—he had to pull it off first. Instead, he focused on the releases, keeping his body straight and feeling the way his hand swiveled around the bar. It was always there beneath him, something sturdy to count on.

He landed the dismount, heart jumping into his throat the moment he hit the ground, knowing it wasn't good enough, wouldn't be good enough to make it. Dorian said nothing as he left the mat, and that, if anything, made Auden feel surer that his changes in difficulty were necessary to win.

Chapter 17
Trials and Errors

Raleigh was a bright, cheerful city, sunny and warm, but Auden couldn't enjoy any of it, and he found himself sitting in the empty gym after dark. The teams had left, practice long over, but Auden couldn't bring himself to go back to the hotel and crawl into bed. Tomorrow, his fate would be decided by a panel of judges. Tomorrow, he'd know if it had all been worth it.

He wasn't supposed to be in this gym either, not alone, not after dark, but it was completely empty. He couldn't help thinking about everything. If he hadn't let everything get to him, if he hadn't been so afraid of letting people down, so afraid that he'd done exactly that, he wouldn't be in this mess. He would have been laughing with his teammates, excited for tomorrow.

He still dreaded tomorrow, but not out of misplaced fear. What if he didn't make it? His whole life, he'd had one goal, and here it was. He'd spent the past month trying to forget it, to convince himself that he didn't want to be a gymnast when really, it was the only thing he wanted. Now that it was here, he didn't know if he could even make it.

A door swinging open made him jump up and whip around, heart climbing into his throat. He wasn't supposed to be in there. To his relief, and then unease, Trayce stepped through the door.

"What are you doing here?" he asked before he could stop himself.

"What are you doing here?" Trayce countered.

Sighing, Auden sank onto the bench. "Just thinking."

For a moment, Trayce said nothing, coming closer to Auden but pausing to look around the gym.

Auden glanced up at Trayce after a minute. "Do you think I ruined my chances?"

Trayce shook his head, turning to face him. "I don't know what you want to hear, Auden. What you did was stupid and you can't magically fix it overnight."

Auden should have known better than to look for sympathy in Trayce. "Thanks for the support."

"If you want coddling, go ask your boyfriend," Trayce replied, voice sharp, arms crossed over his chest.

"He's not my boyfriend anymore." Auden wasn't sure he even needed to tell Trayce that, but it came out anyway, a knee-jerk reaction.

"So that's why he was declaring his love to you the other day?" Trayce asked skeptically.

Auden grimaced. Trayce had been the one he saw going into the dorm. "It's none of your business."

"You're right. It's not," Trayce said, dropping his arms. "I just wanted to tell you that you picked a jerk of a boyfriend."

"Like you're any better," Auden shot back. He was tired of being blamed for everything that went wrong. Trayce had never shown any interest in anything other than sex, had never even wanted to consider a relationship, and now he blamed Auden for finally finding someone to be with. "You, Trayce Moreau, who thinks that love is a crock and all relationships fail, who won't even open up to the possibility that you could be in a relationship with someone and be happy. How the hell are you any better?"

"At least I don't lie about my opinions or take them back to make someone like me."

"I never did that."

"Your boyfriend did, didn't he? I heard him. I heard his shit apology and how you just accepted it."

"I did not!" Auden snapped, glaring at Trayce. Anger boiled under his skin, hands balled into fists at his sides. Who was Trayce to presume what he'd done? "Why do you even care? You're not my boyfriend. You're barely even a friend most days. What right do you have to tell me who to date or what to do? If I want to get back together with Shane, it's my business."

Trayce's eyes flashed to Auden's, burning in the dim lights overhead. "Why do I care? Why *do* I care! Because I like you, Auden, and it pisses me off!"

"You're pissed off because you like me?" Auden shot back, too angry to even understand what that meant. These last two months had been one thing after another, and he couldn't handle all the stress. It was one thing to worry about competition. It was another to think about guys and relationships and all the complications that came with them.

Maybe he should just give up guys altogether and focus on gymnastics. After all, it would probably be his only true love at this rate.

"Yes," Trayce snapped, taking a step forward, mouth twisted in anger, but Auden didn't move, stubbornly standing his ground. "It pisses me off because I care about you, and I don't care about anyone. Not like that. Emotions get people hurt and divorced and using their kid as leverage in their fights. I don't want to be like that."

"Then don't be like that!"

"I can't help it now because of you! You got inside my head and you do stupid things to my stomach, and you make me think about flowers and dates, and all the things I think are ridiculous." He grimaced as though the thought pained him. "And now you've got that stupid boyfriend who just makes me want to punch him in the face."

Auden stared at Trayce. This couldn't be happening, not with Trayce. Trayce was the one person he could count on to let things roll off his back, to bottle up his feelings and never let them out. As much as Auden had always wanted to hear those words—in a different context, of course—he couldn't help his disbelief.

"So you're saying this because you're jealous? Because you can't have me now? With a boyfriend, I'm off-limits and you just want what you can't have?"

"I'm saying it because I think you're an idiot for ever going out with him."

"It's not like there was anyone else!" Auden glared at Trayce, blood boiling. Trayce had had plenty of time to say something, time to make up his mind and make a move.

Why did Trayce have to pick now of all times to get sentimental?

The night before trials, the night before everything would change. This wasn't how Auden wanted it to happen—Trayce's declaration of feelings. Instead, it made him angry. Was Trayce only doing it because he was jealous of Shane? Because he didn't want Auden to be with Shane? It was kind of fucked up if Trayce was mad at Auden because of his feelings.

They stood there for a moment, the air tingling around them, hot and heavy with humidity despite the air conditioning blasting from above. He could see Trayce's breathing, chest rising and falling faster than normal, the tension to his shoulders.

"There was me," Trayce said a second before his mouth crashed into Auden's.

Torn between anger and desperation, Auden flailed for a second, hands coming up to shove Trayce away and demand an explanation, but his fingers dug into Trayce's shoulders instead and yanked him closer. For a moment, it was a mess of groping hands, Trayce's pushing under his shirt, nails scraping up his back as Auden moaned and arched into the touch.

Trayce's mouth was hot and slick, lips sliding against his, tongue licking into his mouth. Any finesse they may have had in the past was lost in panted breaths, hot palms against burning skin, the jolting thud as their knees hit the mat.

Auden couldn't help falling into Trayce's touch, chasing his mouth as he pulled away, too eager to stop what was happening. He needed this, this release. Hands tangled in Trayce's hair, pulling their mouths together, ignoring why this was happening and what it might mean. Auden was pissed off and getting off seemed like a pretty good idea.

The gym was silent except the rustle of clothing as Trayce shoved Auden's shirt off. Auden's back hit the cold, blue mat, and he had a sudden flash of realization at where they were. He'd had dreams like this, of Trayce fucking him over the pommel horse, but those had just been dreams. This was the real thing —Trayce's hips pressed against his, hot and heavy, a steady drag of fabric and pressure against his throbbing cock.

"Fuck, I missed this," Trayce breathed, groaning softly as their hips connected and Auden could swear all his blood rushed to his prick. His only response was a breathless moan, and he grabbed at Trayce's shirt, dragging it up. His hands slid over his muscles, his hot skin, moving down easily. It was almost like nothing had changed.

Trayce's hand teased its way down his stomach as his mouth worked over Auden's jaw. Auden's hips jerked up as Trayce's hand slipped under his shorts and wrapped around Auden's cock, already stiff and waiting. The friction was almost unbearable, desire throbbing through his body as he pushed into Trayce's grip.

Auden wasted no time and hastily unbuttoned Trayce's jeans, shoving his hand underneath. There was no time for teasing, no time for drawing it out. This was about getting off and getting off quick. Trayce's body pressed against his — chest hot and heavy — along with the torturous slide of his hand on his cock rough and quick.

"I missed you," Trayce said, breath hot against Auden's cheek, and Auden groaned at the twist of Trayce's hand.

"Shut up," he managed to grind out, grabbing Trayce's neck and pulling him down for a biting kiss, too hard, too rough, but still not enough. Now was not the time for Trayce to say things like that, not during sex when it meant less. He couldn't even think of that right now.

Auden felt it before it happened, the way Trayce's body tensed against his, the moan stifled against his cheek, then his hand was covered in come and Trayce panted in his ear.

"Shit," Trayce muttered, grip tightening on Auden's cock.

Pushing into Trayce's grip, Auden just wanted to come. He wanted to forget about Shane and the mistakes he'd made, abandoning gymnastics. He'd cheated on gymnastics — that's what he'd done, and the guilt ate at him, but here, with Trayce, for a moment, he could forget about that. Here, with Trayce, it was the same.

Heat crashed in waves over him as Trayce jerked him off, quickly, smothering his noises with his mouth, biting down when Auden came. Auden's hips jerked up and he cursed into the empty gym as pleasure rushed through his veins. He felt Trayce's grip slack but Trayce didn't pull his hand out.

Blinking slowly, Auden exhaled and gazed up at the paneled ceiling high above them. Trayce shifted beside him, pulling his hand out and rolling to his side. Auden wasn't sure what to say.

"We should probably get to the hotel before Dorian murders us," he said at length. He wasn't sure if he should bring up what Trayce had said earlier, about liking him. What did it really matter? At this point, Auden wasn't even sure if he wanted to be with anyone. Maybe Trayce was right about relationships — they only let you down.

Trayce hesitated, glancing over at him, and shrugged. "Yeah." He didn't sound too happy but he pushed himself off the mat anyway and straightened his shirt.

Auden watched him cross the gym and sighed to himself. He had to stop thinking about Trayce. Tomorrow was another day, possibly his last day if he didn't do well. He just needed to get out of his own head and into competition mode. He just needed to focus.

Auden glanced over as Dorian laid a hand on his shoulder. He stood staring out at the mat, trying to ignore the scores coming up on the boards for other gymnasts. He was up on the floor next.

"I know the past couple weeks have been difficult," Dorian said, squeezing his shoulder. "But you wouldn't be here if you didn't deserve it. Today's only the first day. You've still got tomorrow. So do your best and make yourself proud."

Auden nodded, taking a deep breath. There was really nothing for it anymore. He had to do what he could and know it would be enough. A part of him was glad his parents hadn't come, glad that it was just him and the team. The stands were filled with spectators cheering for their favorite gymnasts. Auden glanced over, more out of habit than anything, to the stands, the thousands of nameless faces watching.

Someone bumped his shoulder, and Auden jumped, finding Trayce next to him. Turning away, Auden shook himself. It didn't matter that he and Trayce hadn't spoken since last night. He was about to be called onto the floor and all his focus needed to be on his routine.

The floor manager nodded at him to come up, and Auden

stepped onto the mat. At the corner, he paused, closing his eyes for a second, blocking out everything else around him. His mind flashed to his late-night practices, the stumbles and the falls. That couldn't happen here. It had to be perfect.

Stepping onto the mat, he raised his chin and let out a breath. He could do this.

Routines always went by in a blur, each movement drilled into his memory, every layout timed, but Auden felt pressure building in his chest as he stepped into the corner for his second layout, the double twist, double back. He felt the air rushing past him as he flipped through the air, landing with a slight stumble, but he caught himself. There was no time to analyze as he moved into the next element. His movements were sharp and practiced, but it wouldn't be enough. This was his last chance to turn back, to end it how he had practiced with Dorian.

Hesitating, he only saw the mat before him, a sea of blue, and he couldn't do it. He couldn't settle. A few quick steps and he went into the double backflip, feet pushing off the mat and momentum carrying him through, then came the first twist. His body whipped around, legs squeezed together. First, then a second, then the third, body opening up, blood rushing in his ears, and a sickening thud of his stomach as he landed, slipping backwards and landing on his ass. He barely missed going out of bounds, holding his breath as he stopped. Pushing up quickly, he nodded to the crowd, disappointment sliding uneasily down his spine.

On the sidelines, Dorian had his arms crossed and he said nothing to Auden as he came off the mat, not while the camera hovered in their faces. Auden could swear he could hear the thudding of his heart, even over the crowd. He didn't even want to see his scores. Though he'd done well on the rings earlier, this routine, that fall, could break him. It would be a long slog up to fifth place if he could make it. He still had three events left and if he didn't nail all of them, he'd be going home.

Finally, the cameras zoomed off to capture someone else, and Dorian wasted no time yanking Auden away from the others.

"What the hell was that?" he demanded, keeping his voice down nonetheless. "That was *not* what we practiced."

Grimacing, Auden bit his bottom lip. "I know I fell but I can do it."

"That is not what I mean and you know it. You can't just change routines, Auden. Not now. What were you thinking? When have you been practicing a triple twist? None of the assistants said anything. You could have seriously injured yourself."

"I have to do more," Auden blurted out. He had to make Dorian understand. Of anyone, Dorian would, right? "I have to be better. I know you want us to be safe but this is my only chance, Coach. I can stick that landing. I've done it before. I've been working on it. If I can up my difficulty level, I can make the team."

"At what cost?" Dorian asked seriously. "You'll get marked down for the falls. You could hurt yourself and end it all right there because you want to try something new. It's not worth it. Stick with the routines we worked on and you will make it. You have to believe in your abilities."

"I do," Auden insisted, though something deep inside rumbled at the thought.

Dorian shook his head, as though disappointed. "I don't want you to sacrifice your spot out of fear. Don't change your routines."

Be safe was what Dorian meant, but Auden had played it safe for too long. He'd chosen Shane over gymnastics when things had gotten hard. He'd let it slip through his fingers. Could he do that again? Or was Dorian right and was changing his routine now a suicide mission?

Turning back to the floor, Auden sighed. There was only one more day left. Floor was his last event for the day, and he'd have to wait until tomorrow for the vault, pommel horse, and high bar. It just meant another sleepless night. There were only five spots available. When it came down to it, not everyone could make the team.

"You're in eighth place," Dorian said, shaking Auden out of his thoughts.

"Eighth?" Auden felt his heart drop. Moving up was a lot harder than dropping down.

"Tomorrow, you've got pommel horse, your best event. Don't give up now."

Auden wasn't planning on it. "Thanks, Coach."

Dorian nodded and moved off to talk to Trayce before he went up. Auden watched Trayce shake out his hands, bouncing up on his toes the way he always did before an event, as though he just couldn't keep all his energy inside. Auden turned from him. He had one more day to make the team and that was all he wanted to focus on.

Chapter 18
Last Shot

Auden dried his hair as he sat on the locker room bench, barely paying attention to the guys walking around in towels. His mind was a jumble of thoughts—bouncing between competition, Shane, and Trayce.

"Eighth place isn't that bad," Liam said, coming out of the shower and grabbing his warm-up pants.

Auden shook his head. "You're in sixth place. Of course you can say that."

"Eighth is good enough for an alternate position," Liam pointed out.

"Only if they take more than two, and I don't want to be an alternate. Besides, we all know standings change like that. Eighth place could become twelfth after one mistake tomorrow."

"Well, if you eat mat like you did today, yeah," Liam replied, but Auden didn't care what he thought. "I can't believe Dorian didn't ream you for changing the routine."

"You can't win without taking chances."

"You could also snap your neck." Liam pulled on his shirt and tossed the towel in the basket by the wall. He looked up as Trayce came around the corner. "Trayce, here, has just got to hold onto his spot."

Trayce smiled briefly, avoiding Auden's gaze. "Don't worry. I don't plan on dropping out of the top five."

"Like Auden said, standings can change in a second."

Auden glanced up at Trayce, but Trayce merely shrugged in response. Auden wasn't worried about Trayce's standing, and his own was out of his control until tomorrow. He just hoped he had made the right decision. Liam was right; it was dangerous to change a routine without ample time to practice. It could end in disaster.

"I'm starving," Liam said, "let's get some dinner."

Auden rose from the bench, tossing his towel away and following Trayce and Liam out of the locker room. Outside, the sun sunk slowly in the west, warm and humid still as it fell over the pathway beyond the gym. Auden let Liam and Trayce go ahead, absorbed in their own conversation, and he was glad not to be involved. There was too much to think about.

His phone pinged with a new update as he walked, and Shane's face appeared on the screen with, "Shane Kaufman is now single."

The feeling curling Auden's chest as he stared at Shane's picture was something between anger and relief. Pulling up Shane's information, Auden's finger hovered over the delete button.

"Calling your boyfriend?" Trayce's cool voice met Auden's ears, surprising him.

Trayce walked beside him now, Liam disappearing into the cafeteria already.

Auden hit the delete button and shoved the phone in his pocket. "I already told you we broke up. I don't need to explain anything to you."

Trayce brushed back his hair, meeting Auden's annoyed gaze. "Did you date him because of me?"

Auden stared for a minute then laughed, once, short. "You're not the center of the universe. Not everything I do is because of you."

"But I told you to," Trayce said, gaze meeting Auden's, eyes wide. "I said you should."

Auden frowned. "Well, what did you expect? You didn't want to be with me."

Trayce paused, shouldering his duffle bag. Auden kept walking. As far as he was concerned, he'd made a lot of mistakes the past couple of months, and most of them had been his own fault. He shouldn't have asked more of Trayce when he knew perfectly well what he was getting into. He shouldn't have trusted Shane so blindly, but he'd been the first person to show an interest in him beyond his gymnastic prowess.

"But I did," Trayce said finally, grabbing Auden's arm and forcing him to stop walking. "I mean, not in the romantic dinners and candlelight kind of way, but I've always liked you. We've been friends for three years, and we've been fucking for one of those years. I wanted to be with you then, even it was just sex, but it's different now."

Auden shook his head. "I don't want to be with someone who gets mad at me because of his own feelings."

"I'm not pissed at you," Trayce replied, taking a halting step forward but stopped as Auden's gaze hardened. "I was pissed at... at myself. I should have said something."

Auden didn't know what to say. Trayce had never tried to stop him from seeing Shane, had never offered an alternative.

Trayce rubbed his hands over his face, quickly, a rough movement. "Do you know how fucking terrifying it is to realize you like someone? After they've found someone else? Someone who doesn't even care?" He paused, shaking his head. "I know I should have said something, but I couldn't. I was too fucking proud. And scared, even."

As much as Auden would have died to hear those words a few months ago, now he didn't know what to say. It all came crashing over him like a waterfall, drowning him in feelings he couldn't deal with right now. Of all the times to decide he cared, now was the worst.

Turning away, Auden sighed. "I can't, Trayce. Not now. I have to get through trials. Gymnastics is all I've ever had and I'm not going to let myself down."

"Yeah, okay," Trayce said from behind him, voice quiet. "You're right. Gymnastics is all about timing, right?"

Auden didn't reply. Timing was turning out to be a weakness of his, but he'd put it right tomorrow once he made the team. There'd be time for talking afterwards.

"This is the last event," Dorian said as he stood before the team. Sitting on the bench, Auden could feel his stomach twisting itself into knots. It was his last chance. "So far, Trayce is in third overall, Liam is eighth, and Auden is seventh. If you guys do your best, I wouldn't be surprised if all three made it. It's extremely unlikely, but that's no reason not to try."

Auden had played it safe so far—doing the routines he and Dorian had worked on for months. Most of them were at peak difficulty already, but the high bar was his last chance to make a stand. He could tell from the way Dorian eyed him that he was wondering if he would stick to the routine.

Auden glanced at Trayce, who was busy stretching and didn't meet his gaze. Trayce's spot was almost guaranteed at this point, but Auden had further to go. One more event. He didn't have time to think about the night before, about what Trayce had said; now was the time to focus on himself, to rediscover why he had chosen gymnastics so many years ago when he could have picked football or baseball. He was naturally athletic—he could have chosen any sport and been successful, perhaps not Olympic level successful, but good enough.

He hadn't chosen football, though. He'd chosen gymnastics. As he sat there, he remembered his first competition. He'd been young, overly excited, eager to try everything and anything that would make him better. He'd fallen off the high bar on a release and bruised his knee cap, but he'd gotten back up and practiced the release until he could do it flawlessly every time.

Where had that kid gone?

"Get warmed up," Dorian said a minute later, turning away to discuss something with the assistant coach.

"So close," Trayce said as he peeled off his warm-up jacket. Auden glanced up at him, surprised he was still speaking to him.

"You think you're going to make it?"

"Of course," Trayce assured him. "I don't doubt my abilities."

"Right."

Trayce tossed his jacket on the bench and pushed back his hair. "Neither should you."

Auden shot him a look, but he didn't have a chance to reply as Dorian called him up. At the mat, Dorian grabbed him by the shoulders and gave him a rare smile.

"One more chance, Auden," he said. "Good luck." He gave him a look that clearly ordered him to stick to the routine, but Auden forced a smile back and moved to the mat under the high bar.

Gazing up, he knew this was it. Either he stuck to his routine and took what he got—an alternate position—or he took one last chance, made a change, and proved that he could do it.

The first time Auden ever went up on a high bar, he could barely pull himself up, but that was years ago. He still remembered the thrill of his first swing above the bar, how gravity pulled his body down in a barely-controlled swing. He'd felt like he could let go at any moment and it would be like flying. This time, he knew it was like flying.

The spotter lifted him up to the bar and he pulled himself up, so much easier than that first time. Everything went silent around him as he moved, swinging around the bar, adding a twist at the top. Under his hand, he felt the bar, firm and steady. It was there to catch him.

For the longest time, gymnastics hadn't felt the same, but as he did his first release—a Tkatchev, stretched—he knew the bar would be there, and the same thrill ran through him as he hands hit the bar and his body moved perfectly, tall and straight. Momentum pulled him through to a handstand, perfectly still, and he heard the crowd come rushing back, the screams that filled him with joy.

It had been so long since he'd felt that; it was like everything was new, and he knew before his hands left the bar for the triple twist release that it would work. More screams rose from the crowd, and he bet if he could have seen Dorian's face, it would have been a mixture of pissed off and stubbornly impressed.

He swung through the Endo, legs tight through his arms up to a double pirouette and then down. On the back release, though he kept his eyes on his toes, excitement spread through him, warmth through the stretch in his arms. He came up on the release. With Dorian, he had practiced a full-out stretched dismount—simple but easy to stick. It would have been a nice ending to a good routine, but Auden didn't want good. He wanted great.

It was a risk, but he'd made up his mind as he gained momentum, whipping around the bar and releasing. His body soared through the air, four rapid twists, the mat rapidly approaching as his body righted itself and he landed firmly, a tiny step forward, but he didn't fall. A wave of exhilaration rose in him as he straightened, breaking into pure elation.

Panting for breath, he listened to the crowd; their screams filling the venue. He couldn't remember the last time he'd felt like this, the last time he'd known that he'd done everything he could and it had been worth every second, and it would be worth every second of Dorian's lecture later too.

"Get down here," Dorian said when Auden just grinned.

He came off the mat, too happy to even care that Dorian frowned at him. "I'm not sorry."

Dorian raised an eyebrow and huffed. "You're stupid... but that was also the best routine I've ever had a gymnast do." He raised a threatening finger. "Don't leave me out of your routine planning again. You want to go bigger, we can go bigger."

It was a little scary when Dorian said it because Auden knew he meant it. He didn't care, though. He grinned instead and accepted Dorian's brief hug. "Thanks, Coach."

Dorian patted him on the back and handed him a towel. "You did good."

Auden smiled as he wiped the sweat off his brow. He still wouldn't know for sure until later if he'd made it, not until everyone was finished.

"Trayce, you're up next," Dorian called, and Trayce nodded, looking nervous for once as he bounced on his toes and smeared chalk on his hands. Auden hesitated—no matter what he said, he cared about Trayce and whatever happened, he wanted them to be friends at the end of the day.

"You're going to be amazing."

Trayce glanced at him and smiled briefly. "I'll see you in Paris."

Auden sunk onto the bench as Trayce stepped onto the mat and gazed up at the big screen where his scores flashed. It had all been worth it, he decided, whether he made it or not. Definitely worth it.

Three Weeks Later

"Ah, Paris, city of love," Trayce drawled as the bus rolled past the Eiffel Tower. Auden stretched his neck to watch it out the window, still unable to believe any of this was real. He looked at Trayce across the aisle, though, wondering if he'd meant that sarcastically. Since trials, they hadn't spoken much about what had gone on between them. After all, the last three weeks had been nonstop training and perfecting routines.

"Just because it's Paris doesn't give anyone an excuse to find a *belle fille*," Geoff called from a few seats up. "We're here to win gold medals."

The rest of the team laughed. Trayce smiled out the window.

"If one of us doesn't win a medal, Dorian will never forgive us."

Auden nodded. "After everything it took to get here, I think he's just glad we're here." Dorian was probably just glad he hadn't broken his neck after pulling any of those stunts at trials. He didn't regret a minute of it, and he'd do it exactly the same if he had to.

"Well, I plan on getting at least one medal, if not four or five." Trayce turned to Auden, but his smile seemed less genuine than it had used to be, a little sadder. Auden tried not to think about what Trayce had said about getting together. He wondered if they could have, if they didn't have the Olympics, if it might have worked this time. With Shane out of the picture, and his head back in focus, maybe things would be different.

"You're so modest," he replied, and Trayce shrugged.

"I think we deserve it."

"Alright, boys." Coach Davis rose from his seat near the front, effectively ending all conversation on the bus. "We're approaching the Olympic Stadium. For those first timers, it might be overwhelming. For the rest of you, try to act impressed."

The bus jerked to a stop at the entrance and the driver said something in French to the guard at the gate. They rolled forward a second later and Auden couldn't help staring out the window. There wasn't much to see beyond a huge shimmering building looming ahead.

After everything, Auden still couldn't quite believe he was in the Olympics. He was on the team. He had scraped into fifth place at trials, an astonishing jump, edging onto the team. His mom had cried when he told her, and his dad, well, his dad had grumbled about the cost of flying last-minute to Paris.

In the other seat, Trayce stared out the window, appearing just as enthralled as they rolled through a tunnel and past gardens with statues. Sometimes it felt surreal. After everything Auden had put himself through, all the suffering he had inflicted on himself, whether intentional or not, it had still led him here, exactly where he wanted to be.

"We did it," Auden said, and Trayce's eyes flicked to him.

"We did."

"Everybody off the bus!" Coach Davis called as it stopped finally.

Filing one by one, Auden followed Trayce and the rest of the team. Stepping off the bus, he stared up at the stadium. It was bigger than he'd ever dreamed, bigger than any World Championship he'd ever been to. He felt like a kid on the first day of school: filled with fear, excitement, and wonder.

Coach Davis led the way in, down a brightly-lit hallway, painted the Olympic colors for that year — green and white — and paused before a pair of double doors.

"Welcome to the biggest two weeks of your life," Coach said as he pushed open the doors and strode inside.

Auden stepped inside, jaw dropping as he stared up at the huge domed ceiling, shimmering with silver. The mats on the floor were green, the floor painted white throughout. It was like living a dream. This was better than any boyfriend he could have had, but after a second, he reached over and put a hand on Trayce's shoulder. He merely smiled as Trayce's gaze shot to him. After a moment, though, Trayce smiled in return and turned back to the arena. Lights twinkled down from high above and Auden knew it was going to be a great Olympic Games.

Author's Notes

Tumbled picks up where *Vaulted* didn't end—more than ten years down the road. Sometimes, when you get going in a particular universe, the urge to write more takes over which is where Tumbled came from. Though the plot revolves around Auden, we still get to see where Dorian and Jules ended up which is a nice little extra to fans of *Vaulted*. Way back in 2012 when I wrote *Vaulted* and then *Tumbled*, I spent too much time watching the summer Olympics, but it wasn't the first time. As a kid (before TiVo), I'd stay up until ungodly hours just to watch the gymnastic events. Gymnastics has long been my favorite Olympic competition to watch (diving is a close second but even those teeny tiny shorts can't beat out the pure physical prowess of gymnastics) and writing a novel was a logical step. Writing advice always tells you to write what you know. Here's my advice: don't write what you know; write what you love. I love gymnastics and that helped bring Auden and Dorian to life. The Olympics are coming around again soon, and I think you can guess where I'll be. That's right, watching gymnastics.

—E. E. Grey

About the Author

E. E. Grey started to write fresh out of high school, but the hobby grew over time. Now Grey has completed six novel-length works and over three hundred short stories. When not writing, Grey enjoys traveling, having visited over twenty countries already, and baking for friends and family.

ForbiddenFiction works by E. E. Grey

Novels

Vaulted
Tumbled

Novellas and Short Stories

Brush with Death
By the Hour
Checking Out
Cigarette Burns
From the Storm
Stage Dreams

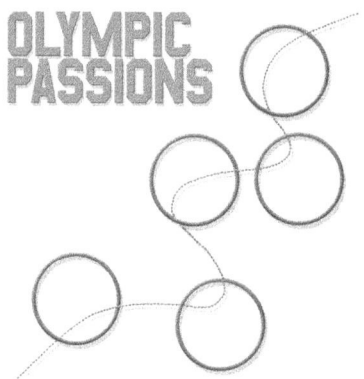

Olympic Passions

It isn't easy to win both love and gold. To be an Olympic athlete requires incredible passion. There are other passions, however, which rise in young men training in such close quarters. When these passions swell, an athlete's dedication can waver. It's hard to keep your eyes on the prize when your friend's finely muscled back is so distracting...

Will it be love over gold? Will these young men choose each other over the Olympics? Or can they find a way to win it all?

Works in this series:

1. Vaulted
2. Tumbled

About the Publisher

ForbiddenFiction.com is a publisher devoted to writing that breaks the boundaries of original erotic fiction. Our stories combine intense sexuality with quality writing. Stories at Forbidden Fiction.com not only arouse readers through sensations, but also engage them emotionally and mentally through storytelling as well-crafted as the sex is hot.

ForbiddenFiction.com is also designed to be a social reading environment. You'll have fun even if just reading the latest post each day, yet you will have the chance for so much more. Readers and authors can be part of ongoing discussions of specific works and individual authors as well as more general topics.

Sign up for a FREE Membership today at ForbiddenFiction.com

www.ingramcontent.com/pod-product-compliance
Lightning Source LLC
Chambersburg PA
CBHW051520170626
46811CB00002B/922